Blake's 7
Project Avalon

The prisoner was gazing placidly into space, apparently unaffected by the contents of the phial. Absently he brushed the back of one hand, as if shooing away a fly, and after a second or two repeated the gesture with growing irritation. It was only when he looked down that he realized, with mounting horror, what was happening to him.

Something was growing on his hand. It was like a fungus, grey and cellular and spongelike, and it was dividing and multiplying itself with astonishing, frightening speed. The man began to claw at it desperately, his face stricken with terror, but now it had enveloped both hands and was creeping rapidly up his arms. And as he twisted aside, in wild-eyed panic, the watchers saw that the grey, cellular fungus had attached itself to his neck and was devouring his face.

Falling to his knees, the man opened his mouth in a scream of anguish, though not a sound escaped from the sealed sound-proofed room. Within moments the struggling mound of grey sponge had lost all resemblance to a human being, not a single feature visible, and after a few slight spasmodic twitches lay completely still, a dead and lifeless mass of fungus.

'Very impressive,' Servalan said quietly.

Trevor Hoyle

Terry Nation's

Project Avalon

Arrow Books

Arrow Books Ltd
3 Fitzroy Square, London W1P 6JD

An imprint of the Hutchinson Publishing Group

London Melbourne Sydney Auckland
Wellington Johannesburg and agencies
throughout the world

First published Arrow Books Ltd 1979
This novelization © Trevor Hoyle 1979

Set in Photomix Times by
Book Economy Tapeset Ltd. Cuckfield, Sussex

Made and printed in Great Britain by
The Anchor Press Ltd, Tiptree, Essex

ISBN 0 09 919340 X

Part One

1

The tense silence seemed to hum in their ears like static electricity. No one had ventured to speak for several minutes, all eyes on the sweeping hand of the large chronograph display flush-mounted into the bulkhead wall as it marked off precious segments of time. Seated at the teleport control panel, Jenna drummed her slim fingers impatiently and turned her gaze to her three companions waiting in the transmission area.

Only Avon gave the impression of being unconcerned. His heavily lidded eyes and slightly contemptuous expression were meant to convey an absence of emotion that was akin to the machine intelligence of the computers he understood so well. But Jenna wasn't fooled. It was part of Avon's persona to project this image of cold indifference.

As for the other two, Gan was hardly able to contain his pent-up frustration, his big square hands clenching and relaxing, his deep-set eyes beneath the massive brow fixed unblinkingly on the moving hand, while Cally paced to and fro with the lithe, supple grace of a highly trained guerilla fighter — and she was precisely that, down to her tightly laced combat boots.

Fully briefed, armed and equipped for action, each one with a specialized task to perform, the crew of the *Liberator* were sweating out the period of inactivity that precedes a daring and meticulously planned sabotage operation. The minutes of waiting were the worst.

'It is taking too long.' Cally paused in mid-stride and swung round, her wide green eyes like those of an animal trapped in a cage. She was of the planet Auron and belonged to a race of telepaths renowned throughout the

7

inhabited systems.

'That's the trouble with heroics,' Avon remarked in his crisp, dry tone. 'They seldom run to schedule.'

'They'll find it,' Jenna flashed back at him tartly. 'There aren't going to be signs dotted about saying, "This way to the Cypher Room".'

'They may need help,' said Gan. As usual the big man's thoughts were directed towards some kind of positive action.

Cally nodded agreement. 'I think so, too.'

'If they needed any help they'd have called in,' Avon pointed out, rather bored at having to state such an obvious fact.

'Avon's right,' said Jenna.

'I usually am,' Avon said lightly, with no trace of irony. He actually believed it.

Jenna ignored him and flicked back a stray blonde curl from her forehead, glancing once again at the hand sweeping inexorably round the chronograph display. 'Blake said to wait,' she informed them curtly. 'So we wait.'

Blake, too, was chafing at the delay. It had taken longer than he had reckoned to gain admission into the Federation communications complex. The place was ringed by security fences and guard towers, and already he had nearly run foul of a surveillance robot, ducking out of sight as its 360−degree high-resolution scanning device swept its baleful electronic eye round the perimeter defences. Now, crouching in the lee of a huge burnished steel tower and partly concealed by a maze of silver pipes, Blake and his small, wiry companion carefully considered their next move. Open ground stretched ahead of them − two sets of spiky shadows advancing across it as the twin suns sank behind the jumble of towers and spheres in the distance, throwing an eerie red twilight over everything. Vila didn't like it one bit. The colour reminded him of fresh blood.

Blake, kept his voice low. 'As far as I can tell we're in

the outer compound. The top security section should be in that direction. Stay close to me and move in the shadows.'

He started to edge forward and Vila grabbed his arm.

'Why don't I stay here and keep watch?' Vila suggested in a hopeful whisper, his bright button eyes filled with wily caution.

But Blake had no time to entertain Vila's noted instinct for self-preservation, and with a terse, 'Come on,' he launched himself from out of the shadows and ran swiftly across the open ground, his broad powerful frame bent low, his dark eyes alert for Federation guards or the return of the patrolling robot. Vila sighed and reluctantly followed.

In seconds they had reached the protective cover of a low concrete blockhouse, beyond which a short roadway gave access to a high security gate. Flanking the gate, the end wall of a building with a metal door. Everything was locked and barred, totally secure. It wasn't going to be easy.

Blake stared thoughtfully at the gate. 'That must be the way in. Can you open it or do we have to go over?'

Locked doors and gates were Vila's speciality. He hadn't come across one he couldn't open — given time. He gave the gate a professional scrutiny and offered his expert opinion. 'You won't get over it. It'll have every detector device you can imagine and a few more besides.' He clicked his tongue. 'I'll have to get a closer look at the locking system.'

'All right, go to it. I'll watch the roadway.'

Vila skipped nimbly across, happier now that he was faced with something that required his special talent. He gave the metal door only a cursory examination — as he had assumed it was firmly locked — and turned his attention to a panel mounted in a free-standing console a metre or so from the gate. From his arm pouch Vila took a silver-tipped probe and began an inspection of the circuitry. The locking system was new to him and he proceeded with caution; not cautiously enough, however, for as he touched one of the terminals there was a brief glare of intense light and a puff of blue smoke. The probe had fused into a wilting molten blob. With a slight shrug, Vila carried on with his examination. He was always willing to learn.

Blake had positioned himself at the corner of the concrete blockhouse, a vantage point that gave him the maximum observation of the approach to the gate and inner compound. Even so, it was the sound that first alerted him — a low-pitched beeping at two-second intervals — and then the robot came into view, its scanning eye rotating in the smooth, tapered dome, its squat body bristling with detection antenna and anti-personnel weaponry.

'Vila!' Blake called, as loudly as he dared. 'Take cover!'

'Uh huh,' Vila responded absently, intent now on the intriguing problem before him. A new type of locking system was always a challenge.

Blake pressed back out of sight. If he broke cover the robot would almost certainly register his presence; Vila was in full view and he could do nothing. Still trying to attract his attention, Blake retreated to the rear of the blockhouse and disappeared.

Approaching on its pre-set route, the robot turned the corner and came steadily on, its scanning electronic eye making a slow sweep along the fence . . . past the gate and the building with the metal door . . . and then it turned and continued on its way, the beeps growing fainter as it vanished amongst the towers and spheres of the complex.

Blake stepped out of hiding, his rugged features baffled. He ran his hand through the dark curly hair at the nape of his neck as he surveyed the deserted roadway, then walked quickly across to the gate. Where had Vila got to? One minute he had been out in the open, without any cover, and the next he had disappeared.

'Vila?' Blake called softly, looking round in consternation.

The metal door in the end of the building opened and out popped Vila's head, eyebrows raised to the flat cap of hair. 'Has it gone?'

'How did you get in there?'

'There isn't a lock I can't open,' Vila informed him cheerfully, 'if I'm scared enough.'

Blake indicated the gate's locking system. 'Are you scared enough for that one?'

'What do you think?'

Vila went to work on the panel using the small toolkit he had taken from inside his jerkin and in a moment had exposed the electronic guts of the console, a compact array of solid-state circuitry. As he worked he explained, 'Anybody authorized to go through the gate has a physio-psycho pattern registered in the central computer. When he wants to go through, this device scans him and feeds the reading back to the computer. If the pattern checks, the gate opens.'

'Sounds foolproof,' Blake mused, admiring Vila's handiwork and at the same time keeping a sharp eye on the approach road.

'You have to intercept the feedback from the computer and convert a refusal signal into a recognition pattern,' Vila informed him, stepping back and indicating that Blake should position himself in front of the console. 'Now, press the scan button.'

Blake did so and a brief green glow lit up his face. Vila ticked off the seconds on his fingers, intoning the sequence as he did so:

'Retrieval system . . . no record found . . . refusal signal reinterpreted . . . recognition pattern confirmed . . . now!'

From the gate came a distinct *clunk* as the bolt shot back and the gate swung slowly open.

'Nice going.'

Vila shrugged modestly. 'Any very talented person could have done it.'

Their main objective was easily identifiable, for there were two Federation guards on duty at the entrance. Getting past them without raising the alarm was going to be a problem. Perhaps the most obvious way would be the easiest . . .

Both guards saw Vila at once, sauntering towards them

as if taking a morning constitutional. They stiffened and peered at him through their tinted visors, clasping their weapons more tightly as the small trim figure strolled up to them and nodded in a friendly fashion.

'Hello there! I was wondering if you could help me. I'm an escaped prisoner. I *was* a thief but lately I've become interested in sabotage. Only in a small way, you understand, nothing too ambitious. I hate vulgarity, don't you? Anyway, I've come to blow something up — what do you think would be most suitable?'

Vila grinned jauntily and stood with arms folded, enjoying the look of startled incredulity on the guards' faces. Only now were they beginning to react, like slow befuddled animals, and as they towered over him in their tight black leather uniforms Blake ghosted up behind and chopped one of them cleanly in the back of the neck. As he fell and the other guard half-turned in surprise, Vila delivered a blow to his stomach and Blake caught him on the side of the jaw with a blow that sent him sprawling. It was all over in seconds. Working as an efficient, practised team, Blake and Vila dragged the bodies inside the entrance and dumped them in a corner behind the door.

'Start looking,' Blake ordered as the two of them set off down the corridor, glancing through the small glass panels in the doors. The first half-dozen rooms were empty, but then Vila halted and beckoned Blake across. Together they peered through a panel and saw three technicians busily engaged amidst complex banks of communications equipment. A guard lounged against a workbench, his weapon held carelessly in the crook of his arm.

'This is it,' Blake said in an undertone. 'Ready?'

At Vila's nod they drew their sidearms, released the safety catches, and burst in on the unsuspecting men. Prell, the senior technician, dropped the instrument he was holding and staggered back, his mouth gaping. None of his companions, not even the lax guard, had time to gather their wits before they found themselves covered by two powerful-looking handguns. The expression on Blake's face left no doubt that they wouldn't hesitate to use them.

'Over there and face the wall,' Blake rapped, herding them further into the room. Vila snaked forward and disarmed the guard, tossing the weapon behind him and pushing the guard in the small of the back to emphasize the point.

Blake held his wrist communicator close to his mouth. 'This is Blake. We've found it. Jenna, get an absolute locator fix on my signal. As soon as you're set, put the others down.'

Vila grinned at him and mimed the action of wiping his brow, his cheeks puffed out in mock relief. But Blake knew they were only halfway there: the vital part of the operation had yet to come.

On board *Liberator* the rest of the crew were making final preparations. At the teleport control panel, Jenna was intent on fixing Blake's precise location and locking on to the grid. She moved the blue circle of light across the graph to align it with the glowing spot that marked Blake's position.

'It had better be right,' Avon murmured, watching her with his pale expressionless eyes. 'A fraction out and you could put us down in the middle of the security barracks.'

'Don't tempt me,' Jenna rejoined shortly, and then spoke into the transmit grille. 'Blake, give me a voice check.'

Through the speaker, Blake's disembodied voice chanted: 'Reading out . . . one . . . two . . . three . . . four . . .'

'All right, I've got it. Locked on,' Jenna confirmed crisply. She took a breath and looked up at the others. 'Everybody set? Here we go, then. Good luck.'

Gripping the slide control she moved it smoothly forward, her poised and flawless face with its high cheekbones bathed in reflected light as the transmission area shimmered and the three figures suddenly distorted and then broke up into horizontal fragments that vanished in a trice.

Instantaneously they materialized in the Cypher Room, much to Blake's relief, and not least their own. Getting a

13

precise locator fix over such a distance was always hazardous.

'Down and safe,' Blake reported into his communicator. 'Well done, Jenna.' There was no further time for self-congratulation. Blake issued orders rapidly. 'Vila, back to the main entrance and keep the door covered. Gan, get the prisoners out of here. Find a place to hold them. Cally, you stay with them and keep them quiet. Gan, when you've done that, start setting charges and then get back here. Right, snap to it.'

When the room had been cleared, Blake and Avon began examining the banks of instrumentation, swiftly checking each panel in search of one specific piece of equipment. It had to be there somewhere and they had to find it fast. Avon's genius for electronics didn't let him down, and with a brief smile of satisfaction he found what they were after.

'Blake — this is it.'

'You're sure?'

'It's been updated since the last one I saw, but it's still the same basic instrument,' Avon affirmed confidently.

It was a slender, metallic tube, less than a metre in length, with a row of keys and perspex lights inset into the polished surface. The tube was mounted and fixed by retaining bolts into a large grey console, the keys uppermost so they could be operated in situ. They were going to a lot of effort and putting themselves at risk for something so innocuous-looking, Blake realized, but its value would be incalculable.

'Right. Let's disconnect it.'

Gan and Cally had found a convenient storage room along the corridor, and they hustled the prisoners inside. Lining them up facing some metal racks on which a jumble of equipment was littered, Gan stepped back and turned to the slim, athletic girl at his side. 'Can you handle it, Cally?'

Her nod was cool and confident, her handgun trained to cover the four prisoners, and Gan didn't waste another second. Back in the corridor, he took six flat suction discs from his hip-pouch and began placing them at intervals along the walls. Each charge incorporated a timing mechanism which Gan wound and set, carefully checking that the timer was operational before moving on to the next. Four minutes, Blake had said. He hoped it was enough.

Avon had removed the top panel on the console and was now at work on the interior, disconnecting the wiring from the underside of the tube. Blake glanced up as Gan entered, his dark eyes appraising the big man expectantly.

'I've set charges all along the corridor wall — '.

'Right. Put a couple in here.'

'Two?' Gan said, surprised. 'One should do it.'

Blake's tone was cold and calculating. 'I want total destruction. Everything pulverized so that nothing can be identified. If they go through the debris and find that the Cypher machine has gone they'll simply change their code system and we'll have wasted our time.'

At the main entrance, Vila was keeping a careful watch over the approach road to the building. Once he had been alarmed to see a surveillance robot, glimpsed for a moment in the distance, but it had gone on its way without registering their presence. Still keenly alert, his full attention directed outside, he failed to see a slight movement as one of the guards began to regain consciousness. Sliding stealthily along the wall, the guard reached up towards a red alarm button, and in that same instant Vila caught the blur of the guard's upraised hand and dived towards him. Too late. The gloved fingers found the button and there came the immediate wail of sirens, just as Vila got to him and knocked him senseless. Other sirens took up the cacophony, and as Vila retreated along the corridor he heard the clatter of boots and the ominous beep of the robot growing louder as it turned towards them.

Blake, his jaw set grimly, called to Avon above the racket. 'How are you doing?'

Avon's face was damp with sweat. 'The feeds are disconnected, but I can't get the tube free,' he panted, struggling with both hands to release it.

'Let me try.' Gan strode across and began tearing the console apart. Under the pressure of his incredible strength the metal sides began to bend and buckle.

Near the door, Blake saw that the timer on one of the charges had less than a minute to run. 'You'll have to make it fast!' he barked, and leapt aside as Vila hurtled into the room backwards, still exchanging fire with the Federation guards alerted by the siren.

Blake slammed the bolt home, locking the door. 'We need to block that viewing port,' he said through clenched teeth, seeing the glint of a visor through the small window. As Avon and Vila hauled a metal cabinet across the floor, Blake raised his sidearm and fired at point-blank range. The window burst outwards under the impact and the guard's head vanished out of sight.

Gan was straining to release the Cypher tube, which was still held by a single retaining bolt. He took a huge breath and exerted all his strength, wrenching at the tube with his massive hands.

'Stand by, Jenna,' Blake rapped into his communicator. 'We're going to have to get out fast!'

At the first wail of the siren, Cally had backed into the corner, using a heavy metal table as cover, trying to watch the prisoners and at the same time keep an eye on the door. Moments later the clatter of boots sounded in the corridor, diverting her attention, and Prell saw his chance. Grabbing a heavy metal component from the shelf in front of him he spun round and threw it hard, deflecting her sidearm, and at once the others were upon her, two of them grabbing her shoulders while Prell and the guard disarmed her and removed her gunbelt.

'Watch her!' Prell rasped at the guard, handing him the gun attached to the power unit in the belt. 'You two, come with me.'

As they went out Cally slumped against the table, all the fight knocked out of her, and the guard grinned mirthlessly behind the tinted visor. He relaxed slightly and out of nowhere Cally's tightly laced combat boot swept

16

the gun aside, and she launched herself at him with a diving leap that took the breath out of his lungs. The struggle was fierce, at close quarters, the way Cally had been trained to fight. The guard came at her and managed to get a grip on her wrist, and as the girl pivoted on one hip, throwing him off balance, his fingers clawed the teleport bracelet loose, and it went spinning out of sight under the table. Under his own momentum the guard crashed back against the storage rack, dislodging several shelves piled with equipment, and fell with the whole lot on top of him. Desperately, Cally went down on her knees, searching for the bracelet, the panic rising in her chest as she flung the scattered equipment out of her way.

With a final heave, Gan had succeeded in freeing the Cypher tube. Avon looked at the timer and then at Blake. 'Thirty seconds.'

The door was nearly giving way under the onslaught of the Federation guards. 'Time to get out of here,' Blake suggested, and spoke into the communicator. 'Bring us up, Jenna.'

Her response was almost immediate. With Gan clutching the Cypher tube to his chest, the group shimmered and fragmented, dematerializing as the timing mechanism ticked the final few seconds to zero.

For Cally, events crowded in with frightening suddenness. She had spotted the bracelet lying amongst the cluttered pieces of equipment. Reaching for it, her hand was within inches of the precious bracelet when the charges went off. The explosion blew the door of the storage room off its hinges and half the roof caved in. The metal shelving collapsed and the walls shuddered, sending dust and debris everwhere in a choking cloud.

Underneath it all, her lifeless upturned hand next to the empty bracelet, Cally lay in a crumpled heap as the dust filtered gently into her open mouth.

Jenna had never been so relieved to see anyone. As they materialized she hurried across, smiling thankfully. 'You got it!' she exclaimed, seeing the metallic tube Gan was

17

nursing like a new-born baby.

'It was close, though,' said Gan, shaking his head.

'Too close.' Avon spoke angrily through tight lips.

Blake was already heading for the Flight Deck. 'We're not out of it yet,' he reminded them. 'They'll be launching interceptors.'

Avon turned a baleful eye in Vila's direction. 'You were supposed to hold them off in the corridor!'

'And you were supposed to disconnect that thing,' Vila shot back. He was in no mood to be lectured. 'Not rely on Gan to tear it loose with his teeth.'

'I didn't use my teeth,' Gan replied imperturbably, determined that he wasn't going to be drawn into their petty recriminations.

On the Flight Deck, Blake had issued new instructions to Zen, the ship's master computer. As he turned away, feeling the massive surge of power as *Liberator* accelerated into deep space, Zen's curved fascia glimmered once more into life and the sequence of lights changed. Blake halted, listening to the cultured, rather expressionless voice that always reminded him of a bored newscaster.

'Detectors confirm massive launch of long-range interceptors. They have locked on to Liberator's course and are in pursuit.'

'How long before we outrun them?'

'Battle computers estimate seven hours to outrange interceptor tracking systems.'

Zen might have been giving him a weather report, Blake thought sourly. 'Maintain optimum evasion strategy,' he ordered, already on his way back to the teleport section. At least they were free and running, and with *Liberator*'s vast power resources there was nothing in the known Universe that could come anywhere near them for speed, let alone match them. The fact that they possessed the most advanced and sophisticated spacecraft ever created was the ace card in their hand, Blake realized, and he never ceased thanking his lucky stars for

18

this glittering prize. With *Liberator* and his crew of six — together making Blake's Seven — they had a real chance of hitting the Federation where it hurt most and of overturning the corrupt regime that had outlawed him from planet Earth. Blake had sworn vengeance, and he would never rest until once again the Administration was in the hands of decent, honest men.

Avon was explaining the function of the Cypher component to the others when Blake returned to the teleport section.

' . . . so that all communication between Federation units is sent by hyperspace sub-beam. Messages are converted into zeta-3 particles and then scrambled. They in turn become a totally unbreakable code.'

'Unbreakable unless you have one of those,' Blake interjected.

Avon's eyes gleamed faintly. The only time he displayed any passion was when talking about complex electronics. 'When I get it hooked into our communications set-up we'll be able to intercept and read every message the Federation puts out.'

Jenna raised a finely arched eyebrow at Blake. 'Any sign of the interceptors?'

'We've picked up a whole flock of them,' Blake answered, his tone vaguely mocking. 'We'll outrun them in seven hours.'

'It's almost too easy, isn't it?' Jenna grinned, her clear hazel eyes alive with amusement. She was a very beautiful girl, capable and intelligent, and Blake appreciated all of her qualities.

He smiled back at her. 'Yes — so I suggest we get back to business and keep it that way. Avon, will you make a start with the Cypher device? Cally can work with you — ' Blake glanced round, a puzzled frown on his face. 'Where is Cally, by the way?'

Vila shrugged his narrow shoulders and looked at Gan. Then everybody looked at everyone else in the sudden silence.

Blake's voice became urgent. 'Has anybody seen her

since we came back aboard?' Another moment of guilty silence. Blake sprang to his feet as the realization struck home. 'She's still down there! We've got to go back.' He set off for the Flight Deck, but Jenna halted him.

'We can't. The interceptors.'

'We can't just leave her!' Blake said angrily, confronting them. Cally was a member of his crew, therefore his responsibility.

'Blake, listen to me.' Avon had risen, his expression calm, his tone methodical. 'If she didn't come back up with the rest of us, then she must have been in the building when the charges blew. She's dead.'

Vila chimed in. 'And anyway the place is going to be crawling with security forces by now. They'll be on full alert — '

'We'd never even make it through the interceptors,' Avon went on, 'If you turn this ship around you'll kill all of us.'

Recognizing the truth of Avon's words, Blake turned in anguish from his crew. Cally was dead. There was nothing else to think, no other possible alternative. He had to live with the bitter truth.

2

The huge silver space station that was Federation Command Headquarters turned slowly on its axis, like a gigantic cartwheel bathed in the dim light of distant stars. It was the nerve-centre for all military and counter-insurgence operations in this quadrant of the galaxy, representing the absolute rule of the Federation over countless star systems. Its Supreme Commander was Servalan. That she had achieved a position of such immense authority amazed those who met her for the first time. They were taken aback by her youth, her elfin beauty, her slender, boyish figure that seemed strangely at odds with the total power she wielded and the onerous responsibilities of high office. But she had been groomed from birth, trained as both skilled military strategist and deviously clever administrator, and no one was left in any doubt as to her ability after a single encounter with this ice-cold, shrewdly intelligent and ruthless young woman.

Certainly, Rontane had no such doubts as he sought to express, as delicately as possible, the reason for his visit. He was a politician and used to the currency of half-truths and ambivalent shades of meaning.

'So you see why the President asked me to come here personally to tell you of his own very grave concern over this matter. The destruction of the Communications Centre has far-reaching political consequences. Controllers from some of the outer planets, whose loyalty to the Federation is . . . shall we say, delicately balanced . . . have been openly critical of the Administration's defence system.' Rontane leaned forward across the conference table, his small, hard, grey eyes glancing to where the Supreme Commander sat coolly poised, dressed in a classically simple, almost stark white gown of pure silk. 'There are even one or two radical voices that speak of withdrawal from the Federation.'

This last was the sting in the tail, though Servalan acknowledged it with no more than a mere nod of her small, neat head. Her dark brown hair was razor-trimmed to a tapering point, revealing the pale nape of her neck, and from the crown was swept forwards in a sleek burnished curve. She turned towards her second visitor, Bercol, a plump man whose perspiring fleshy hands betrayed his nervousness. He was in charge of propaganda and the censorship of any material that might be considered, however vaguely, subversive in nature.

'My department has done all in its power to suppress information about Blake and his actions. There is a total blackout on all reports concerning him.' Bercol lifted the rounded bulk of his shoulders in rather a timid shrug. 'But still the stories get out. They spread by word of mouth . . . by whispers . . . by rumour. Each time the story is told it is elaborated upon. Any damage to the Federation is attributed to Blake. The smallest incident is exaggerated by repetition until it becomes a major event. Blake is becoming a legend. His name is a rallying call for malcontents of all persuasions. He must be stopped,' he finished in what was meant to sound a defiant note but came out rather feebly.

Both men awaited Servalan's response, the one sweating and fidgety, the other hard-eyed and calculating, the seasoned politician. When Servalan spoke her voice was surprisingly gentle and utterly feminine, with hardly a trace of the tough ruthless quality which lay buried like an iron core at the centre of her personality.

'I share the President's grave concern,' she began mildly, 'and I fully understand the danger of the insidious development of heroic legend that surrounds Blake. But let us keep this matter in its correct perspective. Blake has command of an admittedly superb space vehicle, but he is still only one man, backed by a crew of five. That is all. He is not super-human. Nor is he invulnerable. He is just a man who has been extremely lucky to evade capture so far.'

'With respect, Supreme Commander, we are already aware of the facts,' said Rontane smoothly. 'They are, simply, that with all the resources of the Federation to call upon, this one, vulnerable . . . lucky . . . man is still free to cause havoc.'

The implication was clear, and Servalan's mouth tightened imperceptibly.

'You have some criticism of my handling of this matter, Secretary Rontane?' she inquired with deceptive softness.

'Not at all,' replied Rontane blandly. 'I hoped merely to convey the concern shown by the President when he briefed me for this visit.' He smiled without humour and stroked the wing of silver hair above his ear.

Bercol cleared his throat, attempting to avert a direct confrontation. 'It would be very helpful, Supreme Commander, if we knew . . . ' he faltered and went on quickly ' . . . if you could indicate what action you now propose to take against this man Blake.'

'Very well.' Servalan straightened up in her chair at the head of the table, and her voice took on a brisker, more decisive edge. 'You may inform the President that I am appointing a Space Commander to take absolute control of this matter. He will be exclusively concerned to seek, locate and destroy Blake.'

'Excellent. Excellent,' Bercol breathed, his broad ruddy face wreathed in an obsequious smile. 'May we know the officer's name?'

'Space Commander Travis.'

Bercol choked slightly, as if he had swallowed something unpleasant, and Rontane's bushy grey eyebrows came sharply together in a deep frown. He said: 'I understood that Travis had been suspended from duty, pending an inquiry into the massacre of civilians on the planet Oros.'

Servalan gazed at them for a moment, completely at ease. The diffused lighting lent the flawless shell of her face a serene, almost ethereal quality. 'I have satisfied myself that Travis acted correctly in that small matter. The civilian deaths on Oros were unavoidable.'

'There are other incidents on his record,' Bercol ventured to point out, somewhat hesitantly. 'Unfortunate incidents . . .'

Rontane was more forthright. 'He has caused the Administration considerable political embarrassment in the past,' he told her bluntly. 'In dealing with even minor insurrections he has been over-zealous.'

Servalan raised her eyebrows, smiling faintly. 'Don't be afraid of the word, Secretary Rontane. Ruthless. A dedicated officer who does his duty as he sees it. And he sees it clearly — in black and white. He had no time for the grey areas of your politics.'

'I'm sure you're right, Supreme Commander,' Rontane conceded glibly, rising to his feet and preparing to take his leave. 'And of course the appointment is made on your judgement. And your responsibility.'

'Responsibility is something I have never evaded, Secretary,' Servalan replied, meeting his gaze levelly.

'Then may I tell the President that you're confident the Blake problem will soon be solved?'

'Tell him . . .' Servalan pressed the tips of her slender fingers together while she considered. 'Tell him to prepare a statement announcing that Blake has been eliminated.'

The two men nodded and began to move away.

'Thank you for your reassurance, Supreme Commander,' said Bercol meekly.

'A safe journey back to Earth,' Servalan murmured, bidding them farewell, and remained perfectly still, her face a polite mask, as her visitors departed and the door closed behind them.

'Miserable slimy worms!'

Rising suddenly, her face underwent a transformation, her eyes blazing venomously as she marched to the wide curved desk and savagely punched a button on the communicator console.

'Where is Travis!'

'His ship is locked into the station's flight grid,' came the instant reply. 'He will dock at precisely 18.23 hours.'

Servalan remained standing at the desk for a long moment, a slender, diminutive figure in the large circular room with its concealed lighting and all-white furnishings and deep-pile carpet. It was like a peaceful oasis — warm and secure and impregnable in the cold black reaches of space. Behind the desk the entire wall was covered with heavy white silken drapes, and Servalan went towards them and operated a control. As they parted and moved silently aside, the whole panorama of a magnificent starscape came into view, diamond-bright points of light spreading endlessly before her beyond the curved window. And as she gazed at them, a million distant suns reflected in her wide staring, eyes, Servalan's lips intoned a prophesy born of a burning and ruthless determination.

'Your time is running out, Blake. Your time and your luck . . . .'

'There was nothing you could have done. It wasn't your fault!'

Jenna placed a sympathetic hand on Blake's shoulder and looked anxiously into his brooding face. His entire attitude suggested a weary and morose sense of defeat, and nothing, it seemed, could bring him out of it. Jenna glanced helplessly towards Avon for support, but all his attention was engaged on connecting the Cypher device to the *Liberator*'s communications system. He had no time for sentiment. It wasn't electronic.

'Whose fault was it, then?' Blake asked vacantly, gazing unseeingly across the Flight Deck. 'I should have checked and made sure — '

'Cally wasn't a child,' Jenna broke in.

'Wasn't she?'

'She knew the risks — we all did. And accepted them. Cally even welcomed them, I think.'

'Pride,' Blake nodded. 'Childish pride. Despair too, probably. She couldn't go back to her own people because she was ashamed of surviving when the freedom fighters were massacred.'

'But that wasn't her fault.'

'Shame like hers is an emotion, Jenna. It isn't rational.'

'Exactly.' Jenna looked down into his face, her eyes bright and unflinching. 'So is guilt like yours. That isn't rational either.'

Blake sighed and smiled tiredly. 'I know. I still can't help feeling responsible, though. And it's ironic that she should be the only one of us who wasn't a convicted criminal.'

Jenna shook her head stubbornly. 'You're wrong, Blake. She convicted herself, and you can't live like that, no one can. You've got to make peace with yourself if you want to survive.'

Blake swung round in the chair and stood up, stretching his shoulders. Jenna was right, but the knowledge didn't ease his feeling of guilt. He patted her arm in recognition of her concern and went over to where Avon was deep into the intricacies of solid-state decoding mechanisms. The two men were roughly the same age, though dissimilar in almost every other respect. Physically they couldn't have been more different, Blake's broad powerful frame, dark curly hair and rugged looks in complete contrast to the other's lean and hungry aspect, flat stare and rather indolent, superior manner.

'How are you coming along with that?'

'The primaries are hooked in,' Avon informed him cursorily. 'I just have to link up a read-out.'

Zen's sequence of lights came on and the master computer reported:

'Liberator is now out of range of the interceptor scanning systems. Detectors indicate that warheads have begun to self-destruct.'

'Have the navigation computers lay in a course for Inderman III.'

'Course laid in.'

'Speed standard by four.'

'Confirmed.'

Jenna pursed her lips and regarded Blake quizzically.

'That's a Federation repair and supply base, isn't it?'

'Yes, for their deep space cruisers.'

'We're going to hit it?' asked Avon, looking up from his work.

Blake nodded, grim-faced. 'This one's for Cally,' he said, and then to Jenna, 'Because I want to survive.'

She read his expression and understood.

When she chose, Servalan could be queen of her own personal galaxy — wandering at leisure through myriad suns and planets like some ancient goddess indulging her fantasy as creator of the heavenly spheres. In reality it was a three-dimensional holographic space map, projected into the air to give the startling illusion of solid objects whirling in the void. It was a plaything, albeit an amusing and relaxing one, and Servalan found that she could lose herself in pleasant daydreams, relinquishing for just a short while the onerous burden of her high position.

An insistent *beep* from the communicator console brought her back to the inescapable present and the demands of duty.

'Speak,' she instructed from across the room, her head still amongst the stars.

'Space Commander Travis's ship has docked.'

'Have him report to me immediately.' Servalan checked herself, the ghost of a smile playing on her fine, delicately sculpted features. 'No . . . have him wait outside until I send for him.'

A moment or two later a young officer entered carrying a sheaf of papers and a number of small blue vinyl containers. He stood near the desk and bowed informally. 'Central intelligence transmitted the records you asked for, ma'am. I have the transcript and the microtapes.'

'Thank you, Rai. Leave them there.'

'I am told that Travis has docked.'

Servalan turned slowly to observe him. 'So I understand.'

Rai hesitated, made uneasy by her scrutiny, and went on reluctantly, 'May I speak, Supreme Commander?'

'Of course.' Servalan came towards him, her severe white gown shimmering in the subdued light. 'But why so formal, Rai? I thought we were old friends.'

'We are,' the young man stammered. 'I value our — friendship a great deal.'

'Yes?' Servalan prompted gently.

'Senior echelon officers all know that Travis is coming . . . . '

'I have made no secret of the fact.'

'Is it wise?' Rai asked, a note of disquiet in his voice. 'They know that Travis has been stripped of his rank and authority, that he has no status now and that he stands a very good chance of being dismissed from the service.'

Servalan regarded him coolly as Rai went on with rising fervour: 'He was ordered to suppress an insurrection on Oros. He is alleged to have continued with his attack after the total surrender of the rebel forces. The death toll was considerable.'

'Travis is an advocate of total war,' Servalan pointed out stonily. 'He carried out his orders with meticulous thoroughness — '

'But the man is a butcher!'

'An enemy does not cease to be an enemy simply because he has surrendered.'

'That is the philosophy of an assassin, not a Federation officer.' Rai spoke bitterly. 'I must tell you that there are those among your officers who will not serve with Travis or take orders from him.'

Servalan's eyes blazed suddenly with a cold and deadly wrath. 'And you will tell them, whoever they are, that Space Commander Travis's rank and authority have been fully restored. I have also appointed him senior executive officer of this station. Is that clear?'

'Yes, Supreme Commander.' said Rai stiffly.

'Let them know too that any lack of cooperation — any hesitation in responding to an order will be treated as mutiny. Let them know I have said this! Dismissed.'

Rai came rigidly to attention, the lines of strain showing at the corners of his mouth, and left the room at once. At the desk, Servalan breathed deeply as she regained her icy composure. The communicator beeped and a voice said nervously:

'It's Commander Travis — I told him he was to wait but he just pushed past me. He's on his way up, Supreme Commander. I tried to stop him but — '

'Very well,' Servalan acknowledged briskly, once again in complete control. She moved unhurriedly to the deeply padded, contoured chair behind the desk. Smoothing her gown over her knees, she sat back with amused expectancy to await Travis's arrival. She would have been disappointed if he'd waited docilely for her summons; Travis wasn't that kind of man, which was precisely why he was ideally suited for this important mission.

The door opened and Servalan raised her head casually and greeted him urbanely.

'Space Commander. It is good to see you.'

Travis advanced towards the desk. He wasted no time on ceremony.

'Your aide said I was to wait. Obviously she made a mistake. She didn't know the urgency of the matter.'

He stood before her, feet braced apart, tall and broad-shouldered and solidly built. His manner, like his stance, was assertive and arrogant. He wore the tight black leather uniform of the Space Corps, austere and free of fancy trimmings, its only feature the Federation crest in bas-relief across the front of the tunic. Travis would have been a strikingly handsome man — he was still fatally attractive to women — had it not been for his ravaged face. Half of it was missing. The left side, from forehead to below the cheekbone, was hidden by a moulded black mask, grafted to the flesh. It was part of him, the legacy of some terrible injury that had permanently disfigured his looks and distorted his personality.

His one good eye, dark and glittering, was fixed on Servalan.

'Your orders?'

The Supreme Commander was equally brief and to the point.

'Destroy Blake.'

'Depend on it,' said Travis bleakly, slowly raising his gloved left fist on which three curiously shaped rings glinted like miniature lenses.

'It's working, now let's see how well.' Avon reached forward, flicked a couple of controls, and the Cypher tube glowed into life, its row of indicator lights in their little perspex bubbles winking on. He turned to where Jenna was operating an instrumentation panel with a small screen and speaker inset at forty-five degrees into the fascia. 'Jenna, see if you can isolate the Federation signal beam . . . .'

The blonde girl slowly rotated the central tuner dial and from the speaker issued a scramble of static and discordant signals. Then came a distinctive tone that oscillated with a regular frequency.

'That's it! I've got it.'

'Now, feed that signal into the Cypher pick-up.'

As she did so the indicator lights on the Cypher tube began to flash rapidly in random sequence, and on the screen there appeared a moving dot of light followed by row upon row of electronically printed text.

'You did it!' Jenna exclaimed delightedly.

'Well done, Avon,' grinned Blake, watching the proceedings.

Avon's face was impassive. 'Under the circumstances it would have been a pity if it hadn't worked,' he said dryly.

Blake studied the small screen. 'What are we getting?'

'Routine movement orders by the look of them,' Jenna answered.

'A lot of statistical intelligence,' said Avon, leaning across. 'I'll rig a selective data link to the battle computers. It's all useful background information.'

Jenna glanced up at Blake. 'We should monitor what we're getting. We'll need a rota of some sort.'

'Good idea. We'll probably have a better picture of what's going on in the Federation than the President. I assume there's a recall facility?'

'It's all going onto microtape,' Avon assured him.

'You've done a good job, Avon,' Blake congratulated him, meaning every word. 'Thanks.'

Avon dismissed it with a shrug. 'Now at least we'll know what the Federation is planning — ' His attention was caught and he peered closely at the screen.

'What is it?' Blake asked, leaning closer.

'Just a signal beamed to K-14,' Avon replied.

Jenna looked at the two men. 'That's where we took out the Communications Centre.'

Avon nodded. 'They're having to use emergency frequencies.'

'What's the message?' asked Blake.

'Routine flight clearance,' Avon said indifferently. 'Priority space channel for a ship going in from Command HQ.' He began to read: ' "The Supreme Commander requests that all personnel will give maximum cooperation to the incoming senior officer . . ." '

'Does it give his name?'

'Travis. Space Commander Travis.'

Jenna sensed a sudden tenseness in Blake's posture. When she glanced up at him his mouth was clamped in a hard straight line. 'You know him?'

'I know him. I thought he was dead.' Blake was staring at the screen, his dark eyes deep and fathomless. 'I thought I'd killed him.'

Jenna pursed her lips, catching Avon's eye. Neither of them said a word.

Travis marched ahead, unconcerned about the injured Prell who limped after him, struggling to keep up, and stepped over the splintered remains of what had once been the door of the Cypher Room. The room itself was a shambles. Part of the ceiling had collapsed, and the walls were charred and blackened. What was left of the highly sophisticated communications equipment littered the floor, blown to smithereens by the force of the explosion.

Two Federation guards were knee-deep in the debris, attempting to retrieve what they could from the tangled, unrecognizable rubble. Travis rounded on the unfortunate Prell, his face twisted in a dark scowl.

'What are these men doing?' he demanded harshly.

Prell blinked and gestured weakly with his free arm; the other was supported in a sling. 'I didn't think it would matter if we started on clearing up the worst of the damage.'

'My instructions were that nothing was to be touched. Nothing!' Travis barked. He glared at the two guards. 'Get out of here at once. Get out!'

The men hastened to obey. Travis stood, hands on hips, and surveyed the wreckage, then with infinite care began to examine various pieces of the shattered equipment, replacing each fragment precisely where he found it.

'Go through the sequence of events.'

'I've already told you everything . . . .'

'Tell me again.'

Prell turned and pointed. 'Two armed men came in through the door. From the description you've given me, one of them was certainly Blake.'

'Go on,' said Travis, his gloved hand extricating a broken component that had been scorched by the blast.

'We were made to face the wall. Less than a minute later three more of them appeared. We were all taken out by a man and a girl — it was the girl who held us prisoner in the storage room along the corridor. We managed to overpower her, then the demolition charges went off.' Prell touched the purplish bruise on his forehead. 'We were lucky to get out alive.'

Travis straightened up, his expression thoughtful. 'How long was Blake in here?'

'Five, perhaps six minutes. Not more.'

'He could have set demolition charges in thirty seconds.' Travis kneaded his left fist as he gazed round. 'What were they doing in that extra time?'

'Perhaps they had trouble getting them to work,' Prell shrugged.

'And why did they take you and your men out of here?' Travis pondered, following a private line of thought.

'I suppose they thought it was safer with us out of the way.'

'There's something wrong here.' Travis shook his head slowly. 'Something I'm missing.' Irritably, he dismissed the problem and confronted Prell decisively. 'You have the original construction plans for the Cypher Room?'

'They'll be on record,' Prell confirmed.

'And circuit diagrams of all the equipment?'

'Yes.'

'Good. I'm sending in a forensic team. I want a complete catalogue of every item in this room. Everything must be accounted for, understand?'

'But that could take months,' Prell protested. 'If it's possible at all.'

Travis's tone was menacing, gentle. 'If I were you, Prell, I should make it possible. And I want a full report in twenty hours.'

As he stepped carefully towards the door a guard appeared and said breathlessly, 'We've found something, sir. I think you'd better come.'

Travis followed him at the double, with Prell lagging behind, and they entered the wrecked storage room where the body of the guard had been recovered from under a pile of fallen masonry. His visor had been shattered and his skull split open. Travis gave him no more than a passing glance and shouldered his way through the knot of men who had been clearing the debris from on top of a buckled metal table in the corner.

'Underneath there, sir.'

Travis dropped swiftly onto one knee, heaving aside chunks of concrete to reveal the recumbent form of Cally, covered in a thick layer of dust.

'It's the girl,' Prell said excitedly. 'The one who was holding us prisoner.'

Travis felt for her pulse, then quickly checked her heartbeat.

'She's alive.' He looked over his shoulder and snapped at a guard. 'You — get a medical squad. *Move!*'

'The table must have protected her,' Prell guessed.

'She's lucky — '

'No, we are,' Travis corrected him shortly. He rose to his feet, wiping the dust from his gloved hands, and gazed down at the unconscious girl. 'Her luck ran out when she didn't die.' He swung round, the black mask that shielded half of his face having the appearance of some malignant growth eating into the living flesh. His single eye bored into Prell with rabid intensity.

'The medics are to give her emergency treatment, then put her into a life-support capsule. I take off for Command Headquarters in one hour. I want her on board!'

Prell and the others fell back as the tall, leather-clad figure strode from the room. Turning to observe the girl, Prell almost felt sorry for her. *Her luck ran out when she didn't die.* Space Commander Travis meant every word of it.

Travis stared at Blake's face. With an abrupt movement he pressed the remote-control switch and obliterated the image from the screen and replaced it with a close-up taken at an angle. His weariness and his single-minded purpose fought each other as he lay slumped in the chair, his tunic unfastened, his one good eye bloodshot with fatigue. In front of him, scattered across the low table, lay several microtape cassettes and an official-looking dossier spilling sheets onto the laminate surface. For hours now, while the station slept, he had studied every available scrap of information on Blake and his crew, seeking to digest every single detail and commit it to memory. Blake was human, and therefore fallible, and Travis was determined to seek out the weaknesses of his enemy . . . and he refused to let a trivial matter like sleep get in his way.

Yawning, he shook two capsules from a tube and slipped them into his mouth, then focused all his concentration on the task ahead. By the side of the table stood a portable tape-reader into which Travis inserted another microtape, flicking rapidly through each frame as he assimilated the printed data. So engrossed that he failed to hear Servalan as she entered the shadowed room and came to stand behind his chair.

'Shouldn't you rest now?' she asked quietly.

'There'll be time for that later.' Travis indicated the dossier and microtapes. 'This is everything we've got on Blake?'

'I checked with Intelligence personally,' Servalan assured him. 'It's all here.'

Travis turned his head and regarded her stonily. 'Have you approved my personnel and equipment requisitions?'

'The ships you want — *Starburst* Class — I'm not sure I can get them. There have only been three of them built so far, and they've already been assigned to the Galactic Eighth Fleet.'

Travis wasn't in the mood to be hindered by administrative bureaucracy. 'Then get them re-assigned to you. What we already know about Blake's vessel shows that it's far superior to anything we've got. If I'm to have even a reasonable chance of taking him I need those three High-Range Pursuit ships.'

Servalan made as if to object, but then nodded. 'You'll have them,' she promised.

'What about my crews?'

'Already assigned.' Servalan observed him curiously. 'Why androids particularly?'

'I've always found humans with a high bionic rebuild more reliable. Less likely to let emotion interfere with judgement. Or duty. I'd take a top quality android over a man every time . . . . ' Travis bared his teeth in a snarling grin and tapped his left hand, the one on which he wore the three rings on his gloved fingers. 'Or perhaps this gives me a fellow feeling.'

'Does it still trouble you?'

'Not in the way you mean. The surgical mechanics did a perfect refit. I had the weaponry division make a few adaptations.' Travis clenched his fist so that the rings were aligned and pointing forward, the lenses winking dully in the dim light. 'They built in Laseron destructors. They're many times more powerful than any hand weapon. No, the arm is fine. Better than my own. It only troubles me because it's a constant reminder that the man who caused it is still alive.'

'Blake,' Servalan murmured. 'That's one of the reasons I chose you for this mission.' She sat down, her eyes narrowed quizzically, watching him closely. 'I read all the reports, of course, but they didn't say exactly how it happened.'

Travis looked away into the darkness, the images in his mind's eye still as sharp and clear as on that day long ago. He would never, could never, forget.

'It was early on. Blake had only been involved with the dissidents for a short while, but he already had a following. He organized some raids against our political rehabilitation centres. Released some of the patients who were having indoctrination treatment. I was assigned to deal with it.'

Travis's voice had taken on an empty, lifeless tone as he recalled each bitter detail.

'We received information that Blake was planning another raid. We knew the location of the rendezvous point. I made my plan well in advance . . . . '

' . . . the group had arranged to meet in one of the sub-basements. There were about thirty of us. I was very particular about security. I had my people keeping watch on all the entrances and exits for a full twenty-four hours before we were due to meet. No Federation forces came anywhere near the place. I was absolutely sure we were safe. That night everybody was on time. We were all assembled and just starting to go over the plan when Travis's men showed up.'

Blake paused in his story as the memory ignited the slow fuse of anger.

'They just walked in?' Avon said incredulously. 'Didn't you have guards posted?'

'Of course I did,' Blake snapped. 'But Travis was already there. They'd been hiding in that basement for more than two days. We made no attempt to resist arrest.

There was no point, we didn't have a chance. I told Travis we'd offer no resistance. He just stared at me. Then he ordered his men to open fire. They ripped us to pieces. Everybody was diving for cover that wasn't there. I ran, found myself grappling with a security guard. I got his gun away from him, and then I was hit in the leg. As I went down I saw Travis and I fired. I saw him fall . . . then I passed out. I was sure I'd killed him.'

Jenna watched him unblinkingly, totally absorbed. 'What happened after that?'

Blake smiled sourly as if at some sick joke. 'They did a memory erase on me,' he told them harshly. 'They set up a show trial. Had me confess and made me explain that I'd been misled and that my political beliefs were mistaken. Enough people believed me. The whole resistance movement collapsed. After that the Federation kept me around as a prize example of a reformed character. A sort of Model Citizen exhibit. Only I didn't know that, of course. It's only in the last few months that the mind erase has begun to fade and I can remember again.'

Avon said, 'Can you remember enough to recognize Travis again?'

'The man who murdered more than twenty of my friends?' Blake nodded slowly. There was a mist of sweat on his brow. 'Oh, yes,' he whispered grimly. 'I'll recognize him . . . .'

3

It seemed to be a room without dimensions. Inky velvet
blackness all around, the only source of light emanating
from the life support capsule raised up on a single metal
rod: a long coffin-like cylinder in which Cally lay like a
corpse, securely strapped down at waist, wrists and
ankles. She had been dressed in a featureless grey shift.
Electrodes were attached to her head and upper trunk.
Above her, suspended by a metal clamp, a graduated drip-
feed led to a long translucent tube that snaked down to
disappear somewhere in the region of the patient's right
elbow. Beyond the bright halo of light from the capsule's
interior, glinting in the darkness, a panel of dials and switches, the only sound the low, whining throb of the medical
scanner as it monitored every physiological function.

Cally's head was held rigidly in position so that she
could only stare straight up into the pitch blackness. She
was aware of movement, of murmuring voices. A face
loomed over her, garish shadows thrown upwards making
a black slash of the mouth, the nostrils broad and flared,
and a single slitted eye gazing down. The eye regarded
her as it might a specimen in a test-tube, then looked
away into the outer darkness.

'What is her condition?' Travis inquired bleakly.

'There is some superficial bruising,' the medic informed him. 'A slight respiratory problem. Other than
that she's virtually unharmed. There's really no need for
her to remain in the life-support capsule — '

Travis cut him short. 'She will stay in the capsule. It
makes interrogation more convenient.'

'The medic's voice rose in alarm. 'She's not yet well
enough to submit to intensive questioning. She must have

rest and — '

'Thank you, doctor. You are relieved of your responsibility for the prisoner. She is now the property . . . ' he corrected himself with a humourless smile ' . . . the *concern* of the interrogation division.' He turned his head to look down at her, the empty smile still on his thin lips. 'We shall want to know about Blake. His ship. His crew. His plans.'

Cally spoke woodenly. 'Your words are meaningless to me. Who is Blake?'

'I think you will remember. Quite soon. There may be some discomfort. Perhaps a little pain. But you will remember.'

'There is nothing I can tell you.'

'I'll come back to see you in a little while. You won't be allowed to give your information till then. Who knows? You may even be glad to see me.'

Travis nodded to someone waiting in the darkness. 'You may begin.'

The pale blur of a face floated above her. She glimpsed a pair of hands wearing the clinging latex gloves used by surgeons. The hands were holding something that caught the light, and then she saw clearly that it was a large syringe containing a colourless fluid. The syringe was inserted into the drip-feed and the plunger slowly pressed. As the fluid was forced under pressure down the tube Cally felt her entire body flinch involuntarily. Her jaw ached with the effort of witholding the scream of terror that welled in her throat. Staring upwards into the blackness, her limbs rigid, she felt the fluid begin to seep into her body.

Taking the fragment of perspex between stainless steel tweezers, Prell positioned it on the viewing plate beneath the magnifying lens. Nearby, several technicians in white smocks were sifting the shattered remnants of equipment, examining and tabulating each individual piece with painstaking care, then placing it on the gleaming white surface of the table that had been specially set up in the centre of the Cypher Room. Any items that couldn't be identified were passed along for closer inspection, and it was one of these that Prell was now studying with rapt concentration.

Adjusting the calibration, he peered through the lens, then glanced at the checklist on the bench beside him. 'Strange . . . the surface scoring would suggest that it was exposed at the time of the explosion.' He ran his sterile-gloved finger down the list. 'Let's see now. The coding is – ah, yes: "Relay boost. Prime linkage to component fourteen thirty-one." '

Looking at the labelled pieces on the table, he searched for the appropriate coding. 'What have we salvaged for that classification?'

After a quick perusal, one of the technicians reported, 'There's nothing here. Not a single fragment.'

Prell frowned and picked up the master component list. 'Fourteen thirty-one . . . fourteen thirty-one,' he muttered. His face stiffened and the light of understanding dawned in his eyes.

'Of course – obvious. Obvious!' He turned abruptly and rapped out: 'Priority message to Space Commander Travis. Delivery by Category One courier. Message reads:

Thorough check of salvaged material reveals no trace of parts used in manufacture of component fourteen thirty-one. It is virtually certain that the instrument was removed before the explosion.

Travis looked up from the message slip, delivered to his hand by courier, and fixed his dark eye on Servalan.

'Blake got the Cypher machine.'

Servalan was alarmed. She leant forward in the chair, her finely arched brows knitting together. 'He's able to read everything we transmit – forward planning movements, security, everything – '

'That's right.' Travis was nodding, his face suffused with a strange inner excitement.

'I must advise Central Security,' Servalan said urgently, reaching for the communicator key. 'We have to introduce a new code system immediately.'

'No — wait!' Travis held up his hand. 'If the code system is changed, Blake will know we're on to him.'

'That's not important. What matters is that our security is wide open.'

Servalan's pale fingers depressed the key and Travis grabbed her wrist.

'Listen to me! We know that Blake is reading us. If we transmit a message in the normal routine way, he will intercept it.' A note of cunning had slipped into Travis's voice. 'Now . . . what if that message was something he wanted to hear?'

Servalan watched him alertly, and Travis went on: 'Something that we know would bring him to a particular place. A place where we would be waiting for him . . . .'

The Supreme Commander slowly withdrew her hand. She began to smile, looking up into Travis's cruelly handsome face which bore an expression of sly triumph.

Jenna was bored. Lounging in the padded chair, she idly scanned the never-ending stream of information coming in on the screen, routine traffic flowing to and fro between Federation bases and Command Headquarters. There was little to excite interest — certainly nothing of intelligence value that could prove useful. Rising to her feet, she stretched her lithe young body and shook her tousled blonde head to ease the cramp in her neck. Another hour on duty and then it would be Vila's turn on the rota; well, he was welcome to it.

Reseating herself, Jenna's languid gaze passed over the electronic script unrolling on the screen, reading it with only half a mind. It was a new report beamed from Federation HQ — Jenna came bolt upright in the chair, no longer languid or bored. She read the report again and then stabbed a button to hold it on screen. A second later she was out of the chair and running across the Flight Deck, heading for the teleport section.

'Blake . . . Blake!'

'What's wrong?' Blake appeared before she reached the

door, Avon and Vila close behind, their faces registering alarm.

'Cally's alive!' Jenna burst out, unable to contain her exultation. She caught Blake's arm and pulled him forward. 'She's alive! It's true! Just came through on the Cypher encoder — '

The four of them crowded round the screen, their excitement growing as Blake read out the message.

' "Injured female prisoner taken after attack on Communications Centre K-14 to be transported to Intelligence Unit 5 on planet Centero for treatment and interrogation . . . " '

Vila's impish face was split in a wide delighted grin. 'I knew she wasn't dead!' he exclaimed, doing a little jig.

'No, you didn't,' Avon said laconically.

'No, I didn't,' Vila admitted wryly.

Avon stared pensively at the screen. ' "Treatment and interrogation." ' He looked gravely at Blake. 'That doesn't sound very promising.'

'And look at the flight clearance,' Jenna said worriedly, pointing. 'It's for a deep space cruiser and escort of interceptors. They're not taking any chances.'

But Blake wouldn't have cared if the entire Federation Space Fleet had been detailed as escort. 'She's alive. That's all that matters,' he told them briskly, and turned at once to Zen.

'Immediate course change. Direct route to Centero. Speed: standard by six.'

'*Confirmed,*' Zen responded instantly.

'I want everything from the data banks concerning Centero. Everything — geophysical, political, economic and socio-historical profiles. The whole works.'

'*Confirmed.*'

'And I want it now!'

'*Data banks are collating the required information,*' Zen reported in its precise, indifferent tone. '*Liberator is turning onto new course heading . . . now.*'

The huge needle-pointed prow of the vessel with the three streamlined nacelles fanning out from the main body of the craft began to turn on a new alignment. The hyper-propulsion unit in the bulbous stern pulsed a vivid vibrant green as *Liberator* surged forward, the whine of its engines mounting to a steady throbbing roar as the massive ship accelerated through deep space.

Avon caught Blake's eye as he turned away from the master computer.

'Precisely what have you got in mind?'

'I'm not sure yet.'

From the flight control desk, where she'd calculated the time parameters, Jenna spoke up. 'We've got fourteen hours before the cruiser's estimated time of arrival at Centero. We could move in and make a really fast strike. They wouldn't be expecting anything.'

'They're travelling in strength,' Avon agreed soberly. 'Surprise is certainly the only element we have on our side.'

Blake was only half listening. He was deep in thought, and when he spoke it was inwardly, as if to himself. 'Well, however we do it, one way or another we're going to get Cally out of there.'

He was more determined than ever they'd seen him before. His resolve was unshakable. Nothing was going to stand in his way.

Travis stood with Escon, the Station Commander, at the main entrance to Intelligence Unit 5, observing the deployment of guards and armaments; they were everywhere, at every conceivable point, even on the roof of the building itself. The entire area was a hive of military activity. Orders rang out as platoons of guards scurried to take cover, taking up positions to encircle the building with an impregnable ring of concentrated firepower. Travis tucked his thumbs into his broad black leather belt and surveyed the scene with evident satisfaction.

'Your men have been fully briefed?'

'They're to stay out of sight until you give the signal,' Escon confirmed. He was a tall, hollow-eyed man with a ramrod bearing, a soldier of the old school.

'Right.' Travis jerked his thumb towards the entrance, a blastproof door of titanium-steel. 'I want Blake's group in the building before anyone makes a move.'

'Understood.'

'How are your units deployed?'

Escon gestured confidently, taking in each element of the carefully planned operation. 'The entire area is covered at ground level. Squads on the roof. Back-up units on red alert. Destructors with wide firing spreads circling the building. Every exit sealed off tight. Once he's inside there's no way he can get out.'

'You'd better be right.' Travis spoke lightly, but there was a threat buried there somewhere. 'If there are any mistakes . . . .'

The two men entered the building and made their way along a low concrete corridor with caged wall lights which threw a gloomy wash of yellow over everything. The interrogation room was at the far end, little more than a small, square, windowless cell. It contained a single metal chair connected by a series of coiled wires to an instrument console. From somewhere came the faint acrid smell of chemicals and burnt rubber.

Cally sat strapped in the chair, her hair clinging damply to her forehead, her normally intense green eyes dulled and lethargic; she was conscious but only dimly aware of her surroundings.

'I've had a transceiver installed,' Escon pointed out, showing Travis a microphone handset and speaker grille on the wall. 'You can communicate from here with every unit.'

'Space watch reports?'

'An unidentified ship — Blake's we assume — entered our upper atmosphere about an hour before you arrived. It came in close and then went racing back out. Our guess is that it was doing a fast ground survey.'

'Seems reasonable,' Travis agreed. 'Where is it now?'

'Fixed orbit. About a quarter of a million out.'

'They won't be able to use their teleport at that range.

They'll have to come in closer.'

'And they can't do that without our knowing it.'

'Which leaves just one chance factor,' Travis decided, his expression thoughtful. 'Exactly where they'll teleport down. The odds are against them being precise enough to zero in on this interrogation room.'

'I think we have that beaten, too. My research people have rigged the whole complex with a molecular shift detector grid. Apparently there's an enormous kinetic potentional set up by teleport materialization. It's roughly analogous to the static build-up in an electrical storm.'

Travis grinned mirthlessly. 'I'm always grateful for a rough analogy, Escon, but what exactly does it do?'

'The detector grid will show when and where they land. But more important than that we can use it to create a localized field distortion. While it's working they can't teleport back to their ship.'

Travis nodded approvingly. 'The perfect trap. Easy to get in, impossible to get out.'

Escon sounded a note of caution. 'He still may not come.'

'Oh, he'll come all right,' said Travis, supremely confident. 'He wouldn't abandon the girl.' He flexed his gloved fist, impatient to begin. 'Right, it starts now. Just remember, you let Blake get right inside. Let him find me and the girl before anybody makes a move. Get under cover.'

Escon nodded briskly and left the room. Cally's eyelids fluttered as she roused herself from the drug-induced torpor, struggling to move her limbs against the confining straps.

'You are wasting your time,' she said hoarsely from between dry lips. 'Blake will not risk his ship and his crew just for me.'

Travis watched her craftily. 'I've studied that man till I know him better than I know myself. He has one reliable flaw. Loyalty. He'll come to get you, I'll stake my life on it.' Crossing to the transceiver, he unhooked the handset. 'Any movement from Blake's ship?'

'None. Still holding fixed orbit.'

'I want to know the moment it starts in.'

'Yes, sir.'

Travis swung the chair round so that it was facing away from the door. Leaning across, he operated a control on the instrument console and Cally's body jerked as a spasm ripped through it. Her muscles went rigid, a taut grimace of pain disfiguring her features.

'I'm sorry I had to do that,' Travis mocked her, 'but I don't want you doing anything foolish like trying to shout a warning.'

With a final glance round the room, satisfied that all preparations were complete, Travis stepped into the deserted corridor and made slowly for the main entrance. Escon had done his job well. The approach to the building was apparently normal, not a single Federation guard in sight. But once Blake was inside, caught like an unsuspecting animal in a trap, all hell would break loose. Leaving the blastproof door invitingly open, Travis retraced his steps along the corridor and entered the interrogation room. Gripping the high back of the chair he began to turn it towards the door, his mouth dropping open in astonishment at what he saw — or rather didn't see.

The chair was empty.

'Over here.'

At the sound of Cally's voice, Travis whirled round, dumbstruck. Before he could react a forearm locked across his throat, holding him in an iron grip, and the muzzle of a handgun pressed into his temple.

Blake's voice sounded softly in his ear.

'A trick I learned from you, Travis. I got here first. Take his gun, Cally.'

The girl swiftly disarmed him and stepped back, covering him with the weapon. Her eyes were cold and menacing. She moistened her parched lips and said with a muted yet deadly vehemence:

'Know this. Your interrogators caused me much suffering. I should like a reason to kill you. One small movement will be enough.'

Travis kept very still, hardly daring to breathe.

Holding his wrist communicator close to his mouth, Blake alerted his ship. 'I've got her, Jenna. Bring *Liberator* to teleport range, fast as you can.'

'On our way,' came Jenna's prompt response.

Blake broke communication and gestured to Travis. 'In the chair.'

It took only a moment to strap him in, Travis's arms pinioned to the armrests so that his gloved fists pointed forwards. Neither Blake or Cally paid any attention to the three rings inset with miniature lenses, and failed to notice the veiled look of cunning as Travis bided his time. All it needed was for one of them to step into the line of sight along his left arm . . . and the Laseron destructor built into the prosthetic implant would take care of the rest.

'Don't feel too badly, Travis,' Blake consoled him, holstering his handgun, 'After all, it was an ambush technique you devised.'

Travis curled his lip derisively. 'You're not out of this yet, Blake.'

The transceiver crackled into life. 'Blake's ship is moving . . . coming in very fast.'

Blake checked his chronometer. 'We'll be leaving you in about three minutes,' he said cheerfully.'I should use the time to think up an excuse for your failure.'

Travis glared at him with his single eye. 'You'd better kill me, Blake,' he ground out in a low harsh voice. 'Until one of us is dead there'll never be a time when I won't be right behind you.'

'And if not you, then somebody else.' Blake shrugged indifferently. 'Killing you wouldn't change anything. You don't matter enough to kill, Travis.'

Shaking his head disdainfully, Blake went to the door and opened it the merest fraction, peering cautiously into the corridor. Travis flexed his left arm in the leather strap, waiting for the moment when Blake would move unwittingly into the line of fire. Standing by the side of the chair, Cally became aware of a faint clicking sound, and glanced down with a puzzled frown. She saw the gloved fist tense, the lenses pointing directly forward, and as Blake turned away from the door, stepping into line, the realization struck home.

'Blake!' Cally screamed. 'Down!'

The blast of rippling light struck the wall, showering fragments of concrete everywhere, missing Blake by inches as he dived to the floor. In a fury, Travis fired again, and with a swift thrust of her boot Cally kicked the chair so that it swivelled harmlessly away, facing another direction. Blake leapt to his feet and smashed down with the butt of his handgun on Travis's coiled fist. There was the spurt and crackle of blue sparks and the fist exploded in a smoking ruin.

'Watch the door, Cally! They'll be coming now!'

She sprang to the door, bracing herself flat against the wall, and Blake spoke urgently into his communicator. 'How long, Jenna?'

'Ninety seconds.' came the reply.

'Too long! Make it faster!'

Cally ducked back. 'They're coming.'

The corridor was filled with the sound of pounding boots as Escon and a squad of Federation guards raced towards the door. There was a crackling roar of weaponry and the door was torn apart, peeling molten metal surrounding a gaping hole. Cally tried a snap shot, then darted back into cover as another prolonged burst of fire lit up the doorway in an intense flare of light.

'We cannot hold them!'

Crouching, Blake grabbed hold of the chair and spun it to face the door, then heaved it forward so that Travis was directly in the line of fire.

'Hold it!' came Escon's barked command, restraining his men as he saw the danger, but Travis would have none of it.

'Take them!' he yelled impotently, the veins standing out on his neck. 'It doesn't matter about me! Take them! I order you to take them!!!'

Blake and Cally pressed back against the far wall as the guards pounded forward, and above the tumult they heard Jenna's cool voice'

'In teleport range. Stand by, we're bringing you up.'

The guards unleashed a concentrated salvo over Travis's head, but it was micro-seconds too late. Blake and Cally had gone.

Travis, his face livid, strapped helplessly in the chair, was shrieking with a madman's frenzied rage, 'Don't stand there, you fools! Launch the interceptors! Launch the interceptors!'

The rest of the crew were gathered in the teleport section to greet them, everyone beaming a welcome. Jenna ran forward and embraced Cally, delighted at her safe return.

'Great to have you back safe and sound.'

'Bit close that time, Jenna,' Blake murmured.

Vila was grinning like a loon. 'It's good to have you back, Cally!'

Gan nodded, his emotion written plainly on his face. 'Glad you're safe.'

'Aren't we?' Vila said archly, nudging Avon.

'Yes. I'm glad you're all right.' Avon's sentiment was quietly though sincerely stated.

Blake unfastened his gunbelt and hung it on the rack. 'Let's get to it. Those interceptors will be lifting off any second now.'

Everyone moved quickly towards the Flight Deck, a lot happier now that the full crew was back on board, and Cally caught Blake's arm, holding him back for a moment.

'Thank you.'

Blake patted her shoulder. 'Too many of my friends are dead, Cally,' he told her, smiling into her green eyes. 'I couldn't afford to lose another one.'

Together they hurried towards the Flight Deck.

Already the massive ship was forging into space, heading away from the planet Centero under the thrust of her powerful engines. Blake was under no illusion that the danger was past, that Travis wouldn't continue his

49

manhunt throughout the Universe; but with a ship like *Liberator*, and a crew to back him, Blake was confident he would win through in the end. Even with the might of the Federation behind him, Travis was no match for Blake's Seven.

4

A thin wind moaned like a funeral dirge over the barren wastes of the planet's surface. The landscape was bleak, clothed in yellowish light, no sign of any living or growing thing across the endless miles of desolation. Great and mighty civilizations had once flourished here, a race of humanoid creatures with advanced technological powers, overcome by their own immense arrogance and their unwillingness to bow before the unfathomable secrets of the cosmos. And now, millennia after the ultimate reckoning, the husk of this world remained like a lost and barren graveyard, its cities destroyed, its people gone, a perpetual reminder of the dark demon seed that, unchecked, can flourish and rise and strangle even the most scientifically accomplished species.

This was the planet Amersat: Memorial to the Dead.

On the site of what had once been the largest city, a sheer face of glistening black rock reared upwards, fused into glass by the terrible weapons of the final war. Through a vast jagged cleft in the rock, a plain could be seen stretching as far as the horizon, filled with countless grave markers in the shape of pyramids, their edges worn smooth by the wind and the constant erosion of time. At the base of the cliff, in a hollowed-out space, a single stone monument: the figure of a man holding aloft the two splintered halves of a broken sword. The torso had been honed by stinging dustclouds to an amorphous shape and the head reduced to a blank featureless sphere, smooth as an egg. Nothing else remained of the once great and powerful civilization.

Through the thin yellow atmosphere of the planet, the stars glittered with piercing brilliance; thunder rolled distantly as night advanced, and from nowhere a ragged flash of lighting lit up the sheer black cliff and the plain and the statue — a blinding explosion of light that flickered and died to reveal the figure of a woman.

She was tall and slender, dressed in a saffron robe, her face and arms so pale that they appeared almost translucent. Bare of any ornament, except for a disc, the same colour as her robe, in the exact centre of her forehead, she stared up into the night sky, her face tranquil and ageless, her eyes searching the heavens. She was named Sinofar, and to her had been entrusted the ancient wisdom of her people, the bitter lessons that had come too late to save them from self-destruction.

She was not alone. A wizened old crone shuffled forward from the shadow of the monument and gazed upwards, her skin like cracked yellow parchment, her lipless mouth drawn back peevishly to reveal shrivelled gums.

'Will I never get any peace?' the old woman complained in a high querulous voice, clutching her robe to her skinny chest.

'No, Giroc, you never will,' answered Sinofar, her upturned face resigned; she seemed to possess the forbearance of all eternity. 'There is no peace for us.'

Together the two women gazed into the night sky, seeing amongst the stars three moving points of light, brighter than all the rest, growing larger with each passing moment.

'Are you sure about them, Sinofar?' Giroc asked plaintively, almost in the manner of a frightened child.

'Not yet.' Sinofar was calm, a sheen of pale light reflected on her coldly beautiful, imperturbable face. 'This may not be their killing ground.'

The points of light came nearer, now clear and distinct from the starry background, approaching the barren planet.

The three Federation pursuit ships of the *Starburst* Class hung above the planet like black birds of prey in tight formation. Sleek, starkly functional, with swept-back fins, they were the fastest and most powerfully armed vessels in the Federation Fleet. Every sophisticated device of space warfare had been incorporated into their slim black hulls — and everything else sacrificed to make them super-efficient fighting machines.

In the narrow, confined cockpit of the leading ship, the flight crew of two — pilot and navigator — sat side by side watching their instrument panels with the emotionless, fish-eyed stare that was peculiar to androids. Technically speaking, Android One, the pilot, was female, and Android Two, the navigator, male, but their sexual characteristics didn't extend beyond a mere superficial likeness to their respective genders. Once human, their brains and bodies had been largely supplanted by electronic and mechanical components, a balance that was evident in their dead eyes, wooden movements and expressionless voices.

It was for precisely this reason that Travis preferred them: combining the intelligence and facility of humans with the impersonal logic and dependability of machines.

Seated behind them in the command position, Travis was intent on the forward vision screen displaying a quadrant of the planet's surface and, beyond the rim, a tiny blip of moving light. His concentration was total; only by the sheerest luck had they spotted their quarry, and a wrong or hasty decision now would jeopardize their chances of a successful outcome to the mission.

'Estimate approach speed,' Travis ordered, his lean swarthy face dimly illuminated by the glow of the instrument panel.

'Time distort six,' replied the female android, her jointed fingers punching a sequence of buttons in rapid succession. Like her companion, she wore a plain unisex uniform, devoid of badges or ornamentation, and a close-fitting helmet that enclosed her corpse-white, completely hairless face. The flesh was synthetic, without a single blemish or wrinkle, pressure-moulded to her skull and skeletal structure.

'Minimum scan.' Travis leaned between them, his body

53

tense as a coiled spring. 'Their sensors must *not* register the beam.'

The male android closed down the beam range as instructed.

'Scan complete,' reported Android One.

'Analysis.'

'Identification confirmed,' she advised him bleakly.

'Blake!' A sneering smile of triumph spread across Travis's cruel features. 'The other patrols *have* pushed out into this galaxy. I knew he'd follow this course. I've got him. This time I've got him!'

'Target vehicle maintaining course and speed.'

'Set for orbital compensation. We'll use the planet to mask us from his scanners.'

Android One fed the data into the ship's auto-nav system and seconds later a light glowed on the panel. 'Orbital shift computed,' she confirmed.

'Execute.'

On the forward vision screen the rim of the planet began to loom larger and edge across, shielding the three pursuit ships from the approaching blip of light. Moments later it had disappeared, and Travis rapped out his instructions:

'Put a micro-orbiter above the horizon. Visual scan only. Tight beam link. Make it random pulse emission.' His single eye glittered with a cold and purposeful intensity. 'I'm not going to lose him now.'

Blake and his crew had brought *Liberator* into a fixed orbit on the dark side of the planet. The scanner showed a vague yellowish murk that might have been clouds or duststorms. Jenna was busy carrying out a thorough survey right across the electro-magnetic spectrum: the signs were good so far that it was hospitable to human life, and she reported her findings with a cheerful optimism.

'M-type surface conditions. Earth-level gravity. Breathable oxygen atmosphere. Background radiation is unusually high but tolerable. There's a lot of static too. Place is alive with electrical storms.'

Blake nodded thoughtfully, digesting the information, and turned towards Cally. 'Anything on the star charts or planet listings?'

The girl shook her head of tightly kinked curls. 'Nothing in the data banks at all.'

'What do you think?' Blake asked Jenna.

'Seems safe enough.'

Avon rose lazily to his feet and sauntered across, his flat stare and impassive face as usual giving nothing away. 'What Jenna thinks is largely academic, Blake. We've been running on full power for too long. Slipping those Federation interceptors has used up all our energy reserves.'

'Four power banks *are* exhausted,' Jenna admitted worriedly, gesturing to the red warning lights on the flight control panel. 'If we had to run for it now we couldn't make better than standard by two. And we couldn't hold that for long.'

'Re-charge time?'

'Forty-eight hours,' Avon told him curtly.

Blake stroked his chin, considering, then came quickly to a decision.

'All right, we'll hide here for a while. The planet should give us some protection from detectors.' He spoke to the master computer. 'Take us in as close as possible to the surface, Zen. The orbit can decay in forty-eight hours.'

The curved fascia flickered with a swiftly changing sequence of lights, and then steadied as Zen's monotone issued from the speaker:

'*Confirmed. The parameters were anticipated.*'

Blake grinned at the others. 'I get the distinct feeling that I offended Zen's professional pride.'

'It's just a machine, Blake,' Avon retorted.

Vila winked at Gan. 'And he should know.'

'He *is* the expert,' the big man agreed amiably, folding his arms across his huge cask of a chest.

'That's not what I meant,' Vila informed him wearily, rolling his eyes.

'Oh? What did you mean then?'

Avon cut in, his tone brisk and precise. 'He was calling me a machine. But since he undoubtedly defines himself as a human being, I regard that as more of a compliment than anything else.'

'You're so clever, aren't you?' Vila sniffed derisively.

'How can you tell?'

'I see through your natural modesty.'

'Why don't you two shut up!' Jenna had had enough of their continual sniping and bickering.

'Why can't you be friends?' asked Gan, his eyes wide and placid.

'Friends?' Vila snorted. 'That plate in your head must be going rusty.'

'Yes, go back to counting your fingers,' Avon told the big man unkindly. 'You're bound to get the sum right eventually.'

Gan unfolded his arms rather ominously. 'Your broken teeth would be better practice.'

Cally met Blake's eye and he heard her voice in his mind as she telepathed to him privately, *They have been under pressure for too long, Blake.*

Blake nodded his agreement and addressed them all.

'If we're going to have some time on our hands we might as well go down and take a look at this planet. Anybody feel like some exercise?'

'I'd be glad of some,' Gan said at once, getting to his feet.

'And I'd be happy to get clear of this lot for a while,' said Jenna, flicking back a blonde ringlet with an abrupt, impatient movement.

Nobody else seemed keen to accept the invitation.

'Vila?'

'I'll stay here, thanks all the same.'

'OK, you can take the first watch then.' Blake led the way to the teleport section. It took only a few moments to get kitted up, each of them strapping on a utility belt with its power pack linked by a coiled cable to the butt of the holstered handgun. After slipping on his communicator bracelet, Blake turned to Vila at the control desk.

56

'Try and stay alert.'

'Of course I will!' Vila responded indignantly. 'How can you doubt me?'

Blake's face was deadpan, his tone sardonic. 'It isn't easy but somehow I manage it.' He winked at the others and the three of them strode into the transmission area. 'Put us down.'

Vila operated the slide control and the trio fragmented and dissolved. The operation was by now routine, and after receiving Blake's confirmatory signal that all was well, Vila leaned back in the chair and propped his legs up on the control desk. After a moment he took a number of small plastic discs from his pocket and started flipping them into the air and automatically catching them in rapid succession, his eyes vacant.

They had managed to evade the Federation interceptors, *Liberator* was in orbit near a safe planet, protected from long-range detection, everything was quiet and peaceful for a change. Vila was content with the quiet life; it suited him down to the ground.

Travis waited for Android One to report, sitting bolt upright in the command chair. Absently he flexed the fingers of his left hand and the servo-mechanism emitted a low pulsing whine as the neural circuits activated the bionic rebuild, curling the hand into a tight gloved fist. The replacement unit was if anything an improvement on the original, though he hadn't had an opportunity to test its capability in close combat. But it felt good and Travis was well pleased.

The female android turned her head stiffly to alert him. Her voice was drab, stating facts without any nuance of expression.

'We have visual confirmation, Commander. Target has assumed a stationary orbit one thousand spacials from the planet's surface.'

'Excellent!' Travis breathed a small sigh. This was even better than he had hoped; he had Blake exactly where he wanted him.

Android One had taken a small phial of clear yellow fluid from a bulkhead locker. She turned her body away so that he might not see what she was about to do.

'Be quick with that,' Travis snapped.

The Android was apologetic. 'Normally I wouldn't do it in the presence of an Unmodified,' she said, opening the front of her tunic to reveal a shallow moulded channel between her breasts holding a phial of colourless liquid. With the deftness of long practice, she replaced it with the new phial and fastened her tunic, ready once more for duty.

'We've no time for coyness,' Travis said impatiently. 'I'm aware of your need for Concentrated Blood Serum.'

'Most are. But few accept it for what it is. A functional convenience.' She disposed of the spent phial, glancing at her companion as if in complicity. 'Opponents of Android Modification call us vampires.'

'I am not an opponent,' Travis was quick to correct her.

'It is immaterial, sir,' Android One replied tonelessly. She gazed straight ahead, her eyes like large black orbs in her deathly white face. 'I await your command.'

Travis gripped the armrests. 'Attack formation. Fifteen hundred spacials trajectory. Pursuit Ships 2 and 3 will move to flank. Fire on my command.' His lower lip jutted out. 'Begin!'

Jenna was gazing with an almost dreamlike expression into the night sky. The stars were hard and brilliant, scattered in artless profusion from horizon to horizon . . . and directly above, like a glowing beacon, their own magnificent spacecraft, the brightest jewel of them all.

'*Liberator* looks like a star from here,' she mused, letting her thoughts drift on a billow of pleasurable speculation. 'Be nice to stop running, wouldn't it?'

They had materialized near the base of a cliff that seemed to stretch endlessly on either side into the darkness. The terrain — what they could see of it in the gloom — was flat and featureless desert, about as interesting as a blank wall. Gan had wandered off a little way, and now he called to them.

'This cliff's all shiny. Like glass.'

Blake and Jenna joined him and Blake stooped to pick up a lump of jagged shiny rock. He tossed it from hand to hand, frowning slightly, and held it out to Jenna.

'What do you think?'

'The surface seems to have been melted.'

'Almost like the effect of a fusion bomb — '

'Blake! Jenna! Look at this!' Gan was standing by a small outcrop and peering beyond it into the darkness.

'What is it?' Blake asked, hurring forward.

'I'm not sure.'

Neither were Blake and Jenna. It was a monument, that much was clear, but what it was doing here in the middle of nowhere — and what it was meant to represent — was anybody's guess. Something else claimed their attention. Further along the cliff was riven by a great cleft, sliced cleanly out of the solid rock, and through this they could just make out row upon row of small pyramids laid symmetrically as far as they could see before the darkness shrouded them in a kind of yellowish miasma.

'How many, do you suppose?' Jenna said, a little awestruck.

'And what?' asked Gan, a bemused expression on his broad face.

'Grave markers?' Blake conjectured, shrugging.

'But so many of them . . . ' Jenna murmured.

Gan turned away and then stopped dead in his tracks. Two women were standing near the base of the monument, watching them. 'Blake — !' He grabbed Blake's arm, spinning him round, but when all three turned to look the women had gone, vanished into thin air.

'They were here . . . two women,' Gan faltered, 'watching us.' He went to the monument and walked slowly round it, scratching his head in total bewilderment.

Blake and Jenna exchanged glances.

'Well, they're not here now,' Jenna said.

Gan spread his arms helplessly. 'There's nowhere they could have gone.'

'Maybe we've all been on that ship too long,' Blake suggested lightly, trying to set the big man's mind at ease.

But Gan was really worried. He touched the crown of his head with his fingertips, his eyes clouded with uncertainty. 'Maybe the limiter implant *is* breaking down . . . perhaps Vila was right.'

The limiter had been implanted into his cranium by Federation neurosurgeons as a means of controlling aggressive instincts; it prevented him from killing anyone, even in self-defence.

'I doubt it.' Blake smiled reassuringly. 'I shouldn't worry too much about what Vila says. Unless it's got a lock or it's worth stealing you can discount his opinion on practically everything.'

Jenna was gazing at the smoothly burnished head and torso of the statue, the arms holding aloft the two shattered pieces of a sword. 'It's a broken weapon of some kind. A symbol of peace?'

'Or defeat,' Blake said pensively. 'This whole place is a memorial to the dead.' He looked at Gan. 'Maybe they were ghosts you saw.'

But the big man had forgotten the statue and the two mysterious women. His attention had been caught by something in the night sky.

'Those aren't ghosts,' he asserted darkly.

And indeed they weren't. Three pinpoints of light in tight arrow formation were heading towards the bright star that was *Liberator*. She was sitting there like a graceful silver swan about to be pounced upon by three predatory hawks swooping down from a great height.

'Federation pursuit ships!' Blake gasped. 'They've got to be!'

'Where did they come from?' Jenna asked, dumbfounded.

'They must have been waiting,' Gan said, fists clenched in futile rage.

Blake's jaw tightened. 'The Travis Strategy again!' he said stonily, and immediately thumbed the transmit button on his wrist communicator. 'Vila! Pursuit ships closing on you. Full alert and get us up fast!'

One second Vila was asleep, perched precariously on the edge of his chair, and the next he was on the floor in a confused heap, Blake's voice ringing in his ears over the speaker:

'Move it, Vila! They're right on top of you!'

Scrambling dazedly to his feet, Vila hit the alarm button and a wailing siren sounded through the ship. He ran round in a circle, then leapt towards the teleport control desk, fingers fumbling at the controls. Even before Blake and the others had materialized he was running for the Flight Deck, still shaking the sleep from his eyes. A quiet life, he thought truculently. A fat chance of that anywhere within a million miles of Roj Blake.

On the planet's surface the two watchers near the monument observed the triangular pattern of lights converging on the steady serene glow of *Liberator*, still holding fixed orbit, a sitting target for imminent attack.

Sinofar gazed upwards imperturbably, the ageless beauty of her face like a pale mask in the starlight, the wisdom of countless aeons residing in the dark depths of her eyes.

'They are closing for battle, Giroc,' she intoned. 'The choice is made. We must hurry.'

The Flight Deck was at battle stations. Everyone was in position, eyes glued to instrument panels, hands poised over controls; on the large bulkhead scanner the Federation ships were closing in with alarming speed. Keeping his eyes on the screen, Blake rapped an urgent question at Jenna.

'Can we get past them?'

'They're closing too fast. We'd have to cross through their strike range.'

'Avon, what's our power reserve?'

'Banks five, six and seven full charge. Zero on the rest.'

'Maximum speed and range?'

'Standard by four, about eight million spacials,' Jenna advised.

'We can't even outrun them,' fumed Blake, frustration making his voice ragged.

Vila glanced up alertly. 'We've got the neutron blasters.'

Avon dismissed this hope instantly. 'There isn't enough power for a sustained attack.'

Blake was thinking fast and desperately. 'We'll have to let them get in closer. Try and penetrate their shields with a low energy strike.' He turned towards Zen. 'Battle computers optimal strategies? Limit to three options.'

'Pre-emptive action was inhibited by manual over-rides and absence of flight crew. Strategy options now reduced to one. Battle computers propose surrender.'

Avon stared at Blake. 'Logic says we're dead.'

'Logic's never explained what dead means!' Blake retorted sharply.

'Sensors report plasma bolt launch. Bearing on Liberator directly.'

The atmosphere on the Flight Deck was doom-laden. They weren't going to get out of this in a hurry — if at all.

'Direct vision and tracking,' Blake ordered.

All eyes turned to the large scanner display: a dense starscape in the middle of which a tiny speck of light was growing rapidly in size, enlarging into a fiery ball as the plasma bolt zoomed towards them head on.

'There it is!' Vila's voice was high-pitched with panic, almost a squeak. 'Dead centre!'

'Second bolt launched,' Zen reported blandly. *'Third bolt launched directly.'*

'Put up the force wall!' Jenna implored Blake. 'What are you waiting for?'

'There are the other two!' Gan shouted.

They could all see for themselves. Two additional specks of light approaching on different trajectories, ahead of them the first plasma bolt swelling like a huge supernova as it raced towards the ship, a blazing ball of power hell-bent on destruction.

'It's closing fast, Blake!'

It was almost on top of them, filling the scanner with

flaring light, when Blake gave the command.

'Activate force wall — now!'

Avon threw the switch. The lighting dimmed as the banks were drained of power, and the screen was obliterated by an enormous flash of intense brightness as the bolt hit the wall and exploded. The ship rocked violently, like a small boat tossed in a gale, everyone holding on until the tremors had subsided and the lighting had returned to normal.

'Power loss?'

'Thirty per cent on bank five,' Avon replied soberly.

'Two and three are closing,' Gan warned.

Blake waited until the last possible second before ordering the force wall to be activated, and this time there were two shattering explosions in quick succession, the Flight Deck shaking from the aftermath of the impact. The lighting grew brighter and everyone looked round, their faces ashen, their eyes mirroring relief at having so far survived the onslaught.

Avon was checking their power status. He looked at Blake, his face grave. 'Bank five has forty per cent remaining.'

'Any more?'

'Negative.'

'They'll move in closer now and strike again,' Cally muttered.

'Sensors on full alert,' Blake said crisply, not for an instant relaxing his grip.

Vila thumped the console, his nerves near breaking point. 'Are we just going to sit here and let them shoot at us?' he demanded hoarsely.

'Yes. While they do, they're using power faster than we are,' Blake told him grimly. 'It might even things up. Shorten the odds a little, anyway.'

'The odds on what?' Jenna asked sourly.

'Being able to blast a way through them and run —'

'*Three plasma bolts launched and running. Bearing directly.*'

Blake leaned forward, the sweat gleaming on his neck.

'Ready, Avon?' He glanced swiftly round the Flight Deck. 'Better hang on, everybody. It's going to be rough for a while.'

'I don't mind rough,' Vila said morosely, holding on to his chair with both hands. 'It's fatal I'm not keen on.'

The forward scanner gave them a ringside seat. From out of the dense glittering starfield came three speeding dots of light, converging one after the other on a single trajectory whose point of impact was precisely computed.

It was them. Their spacecraft. *Liberator*.

5

Travis was in a fever of impatience, scenting victory. *Just a matter of time . . .* the thought beat in his head like a throbbing pulse.

'He's low on power, all right,' he murmured to himself, watching the forward vision screen gloatingly. 'He'd have made a run for it otherwise.'

Pressing a button on the communicator panel, he barked his instructions in a staccato voice:

'Pursuit Leader to Pursuit 3. Continue barrage. Pursuit 2, hold your fire.' Then to the female android, 'We'll make him keep that force wall in operation. Bleed his energy banks dry . . . .'

'If Pursuit 3 keeps firing it won't have enough reserve to put up a defence shield,' she cautioned him tonelessly.

'Pursuit 3 is expendable,' Travis snarled. 'Let Blake destroy them and Pursuit 2.' He sat back with a triumphant sneer on his swarthy face. 'Between them they can run Blake's reserves down to zero. This ship will still have full power and we can move in and finish him. It's just a matter of time . . . and Blake's a dead man!'

The Flight Deck rocked and the lighting flickered as the force wall took the full impact of three head-on collisions. The screen erupted in a vast searing flare, gradually fading once again to the dense blue-blackness of space.

Avon wiped his mouth and looked up from his instruments, a pinched look round his nostrils. 'Bank five is finished. Drawing on six.'

'Power projection?' Blake demanded, turning to the master computer.

'*At the present level of discharge, reserves will be*

65

exhausted in two point three hours.'

'Which is when they move in for the kill,' Jenna said bleakly.

'And we'll be helpless,' Gan added, gnawing his lower lip.

Again there came the same nerve-racking repetition, like a constant dirge echoing through the ship, *'Plasma bolt launched. Bearing directly.'*

Blake had to take positive action. It had to be quick and it had to be right. He strode across to the chart table, spitting out orders through clenched teeth. 'Jenna, take command. Gan and Vila, observe for her. Avon, Cally — ' He jerked his head to indicate they should join him.

The three stood together while Blake made a rough sketch of the close space position: *Liberator* at the centre with the three pursuit ships ranged equally all around. The stylus hissed across the paper as he talked: 'It's a battle of attrition. He's trying siege tactics. Our only chance is to break out before we're too weak.'

'We know we can't outrun them,' Avon stated flatly.

'I wasn't planning to try.' Blake used the stylus as a pointer, his voice firm and unhurried and methodical as he worked out the tactical options. 'This is the pursuit ship that's doing all the firing . . . .'

The lighting dimmed as Jenna, in the command position, issued the order to erect the force field. The Flight Deck swayed as the plasma bolt hit and exploded, the three at the chart table clinging on while Blake continued without interruption, not even glancing at the screen.

'. . . it must be low on power by now. It won't be a problem.'

'So we ignore it,' Cally said.

'Right.' Blake jabbed the stylus at one of the other vessels bearing the Federation symbol. 'We go straight for this one. Not under, or over, or around — *right through it!*'

Even the normally imperturbable Avon was taken aback. 'Ram it?' he asked, his eyes widening in disbelief.

'*Liberator* should take the impact all right.'

'I admire your confidence.'

But Cally could see the possibilities. 'It would leave only one more to deal with.'

'Exactly.' Blake straightened up. 'One against one. A straight fight.'

Avon sounded a note of caution. 'If any of our control systems were damaged in the collision we'd be helpless.'

'We're not exactly in a commanding position now,' Blake reminded him brusquely. 'Have you got any better ideas?'

'As it happens . . . ' Avon said, and spread his hands. 'No, I haven't.'

'Then you agree?'

'Have I a choice?'

'Yes.'

There was a pause. 'Then I agree.'

Blake wasted no more time. Turning to the others, he informed them of the strategy. 'Jenna, Gan, Vila — we want to go for a ram. Take out the command ship.' He looked keenly at the three of them. 'I can't see any other hope for us.'

'Neither can I,' Jenna remarked, settling in behind the flight console.

'You'll have to fly us on manual,' Blake told her.

The slim blonde girl was already busy at the controls, eyes scanning the instrumentation display. She nodded thoughtfully. 'We'll have to take the impact on the lower hull . . . .'

'*Plasma bolt launched,*' Zen alerted them. '*Bearing directly.*'

'Right,' Blake snapped, 'the instant this one hits the wall we move. Stand by.'

Avon had taken up his position again. 'Force wall activated.'

The screen showed the approaching ball of fiery light and then the explosion as it disintegrated in a blinding flash. Blake waited for the tremor to subside and the ship to become stabilized before rapping out the command:

'Right. *Now.*'

Opening up the power control, Jenna brought the *Liberator* slowly about on its own axis, the huge streamlined vessel wheeling in space as it turned balefully towards the leading pursuit ship. If ever her skill as a pilot was to be laid on the line, there was no doubt but that this was the moment. A minor error of judgement on Jenna's part and the force of the impact would tear a hole in *Liberator*'s hull, sending the ship and everyone on board her to kingdom come.

Meanwhile, Travis was taking stock of the tactical situation, sprawled in his seat while he listened to Android One updating the logistics profile in her precise, matter-of-fact voice:

' . . . Pursuit 3 reports total power shutdown. They are incapable of further action.'

'Very well,' Travis acknowledged, and spoke into the communicator. 'Pursuit Leader to Pursuit 2. Commence firing.'

'Target ship is under way,' Android One alerted him. 'It's turning.'

'He's running!' Travis grinned mockingly, sitting up. 'There's nowhere to run, Blake.' He could scent the kill now. Within minutes it would be all over. 'Compute their course and speed and lock on. Put it on the scanner.'

The forward vision screen flickered into life showing a single large blip, dead centre, growing steadily larger.

'Speed Time Distort Three and rising,' Android One read out. 'Course zero zero zero.' She hesitated slightly. 'They're coming straight at us.'

'Stand by to fire plasma bolt.'

'Holding course.' Android One glanced over her shoulder. 'Computers propose evasive action — '

'Hold position,' Travis grated, his eye fixed on the screen.

'Still coming . . . . '

The eyes of the crew on *Liberator*'s Flight Deck were also fixed on the screen, watching the image of the leading pursuit ship as they approached it head on. From this angle it appeared as a slim black dart, the starlight gleaming faintly on the bubble of the forward canopy. Blake stood tensely at Jenna's shoulder as she held on grimly to the controls, aiming the spacecraft on a direct, unavoidable collision course.

'Zen — countdown to impact,' Blake ordered without shifting his gaze.

'*Count commencing at forty-seven . . . forty-six . . . forty-five . . .*'

'When he realizes we're going to ram, he'll fire a full salvo,' Blake muttered, watching the pursuit ship looming larger.

'*. . . thirty-nine . . . thirty-eight . . . thirty-seven . . .*'

'Will the force wall hold at this range?' Gan said anxiously.

'We're about to find out,' Blake said stonily.

'*. . . thirty-two . . . thirty-one . . . thirty . . .*'

'There they are!'

As Blake had predicted the pursuit ship had unleashed a salvo of plasma bolts. Ominous spheres of intense brightness racing towards them across the rapidly diminishing distance that separated the two vessels.

'Four of them!' Blake shouted. 'Stand by force wall.'

'*. . . twenty-three . . . twenty-two . . . twenty-one . . .*'

An expression of horrified disbelief came over Jenna's face. 'We're losing power!' she shrilled. 'We're slowing!'

'Full thrust!!' Blake said savagely.

'It's not responding.' Jenna had pushed the power control to maximum. There was nothing there. The power had gone. 'Blake, we're stopping!'

In both ships the effect was the same, as Travis too discovered. With the sudden realization that *Liberator* was holding course he grabbed the shoulder of the android pilot and yelled in her ear:

'They're going to ram us! Evasive trajectory — full thrust!'

But when she hastened to obey the controls were lifeless in her hands. 'The ship isn't responding.' Android One punched buttons aimlessly. 'All systems are locked.'

And it wasn't only the two ships that were losing power and slowing down. Something even more curious was happening. Time was also slowing down, each second stretching longer and longer so that all movements became like a film in slow-motion, grinding perceptibly to a halt. Travis reached out a hand and it might have been underwater, moving sluggishly forward as if constrained by some other, unknown, outside force. He opened his mouth to speak and the words came out a deep grumbling bass like an audio tape played at the slowest speed.

'Boosters . . . full angle . . . trajectory . . . '

The female android shook her head, as if in a trance, and her voice rumbled in a vast deep cavern, 'Full systems failure . . . the ship is . . . dead . . . . '

'What . . . is . . . it . . . ?' Travis said, the words slurring out until they became a long low meaningless growl. 'What's . . . happ . . . en . . . ingggggg . . . . '

On *Liberator*, Zen's countdown to the point of impact, like everything else on board, had been affected by the same mysterious force.

' . . . fifteen . . . four . . . teen . . . thirrrr . . . teeeeen . . . . '

The four plasma bolts had slowed right down so that when they encountered the force wall the bright flare of the explosion seemed to hang in space and only gradually fade away. Rocking lazily from the slow and prolonged blast, *Liberator* moved onward, nosing gently forward until its needle-pointed antennae touched the pursuit ship. And in that instant time stood still. It was as if they were frozen, locked together in a separate spacetime continuum that existed outside the temporal flow of the Universe.

The Flight Deck on *Liberator* resembled a wax tableau, everyone transfixed in attitudes that caught their last movements in mid-motion. Jenna was staring unblinkingly at the screen, her hands clamped to the controls. Vila was half out of his chair, suspended in the act of rising, his mouth gaping open. Avon's finger was still on the button which he had pressed to deactivate the force wall. Gan was frowning, rings of sweat under his eyes that had gathered into motionless droplets.

Everything was as still and lifeless as a photograph.

A soft ambience of light began to glow about Blake. It cocooned him in a diffuse radiance, like a surrounding halo; his eyelids quivered and he blinked with infinite slowness. Animation returned with a dreamlike quality, as if he were awakening from a timeless slumber, and he stumbled a few steps across the Flight Deck, gazing blankly at the frozen tableau of figures.

The aura of light began to increase, to grow brighter, until it blinded him with a pure naked intensity that seemed to strike through his very being. His face contorted with pain, his arms went up to shield his head, and as the light shimmered about him with blinding force his body began to fade away.

The light slowly dimmed, and when it was gone, so too was Blake.

Sinofar stood beside the monument. Her eyes were closed, her arms raised slightly, hands turned palm upwards as if seeking to transmit a beam of thought through the ether. On her forehead the disc glowed, or rather it pulsed with a vibrant orange hue — turned to face the night sky where the two spacecraft appeared like bright twin stars, fixed and unmoving in the starry firmament.

Blake stood facing the monument. A little distance away stood Travis. They were conscious of each other, and of their surroundings, but unable to move or speak. The only sound was the high thin rasp of the wind scurrying across the plain. From out of the shadows shuffled a bent and withered creature, her face deeply etched with age, her eyes like dull spheres of cloudy glass. Clasping her bony hands to her chest, Giroc peered into the sky, her narrow bloodless lips drawing back as she uttered hoarsely:

'Listen to me. Listen to me . . .'

Her voice, thin and dry as the rasping wind, was like a vast cosmic whisper. It crept softly through the *Liberator*'s Flight Deck where the crew had just begun to awaken, looking at each other with the befuddled air of sleepwalkers; to them it was a voice from nowhere.

' . . . your ship is held in a stasis beam . . only your life-support systems will function . . . '

The androids in the leading pursuit ship listened impassively to the whispering voice as it went on:

' . . . you yourselves have been released so that you may watch, listen . . . . '

The *Liberator*'s scanner screen suddenly came on, showing Blake and Travis standing near the monument.

' . . . and learn.'

Giroc turned her dulled and rheumy gaze from the night sky and bowed reverentially to Sinofar.

'We are ready. They can be released.'

As if relaxing from a tremendous strain, Sinofar emitted a shallow sigh and let her hands fall by her sides. She opened her eyes and the disc on her forehead gradually faded, losing its pulsating orange glow.

Blake and Travis suddenly found that they could move. Sinofar smiled gently, amused by their expressions, her face translucently pale and tranquil in the cold clear starlight. Blake was lost for words, gazing at her with an almost naive incredulity, drinking in her perfection.

Travis had no time for such emotion. Only a single black thought filled his head, like an all-consuming mania. Raising his gloved fist with the three lensed rings, he aimed it directly at Blake's chest and activated the Laseron destructor beam.

Nothing happened.

The old crone glanced slyly at Travis, her mouth twisted in a toothless grin. She gave a low malicious cackle. 'The weapon built into that hand will not work here. Primitive.'

'Giroc,' Sinofar chided her, sighing.

'His impulse to kill is primitive.'

'As ours was not?' Sinofar's voice had a sad, resigned quality.

'Who are you?' asked Blake curiously.

The tall, slender woman in the flowing saffron robes

made a gesture, her hand as graceful as a swaying frond. 'I am Sinofar, the Guardian. This is Giroc, the Keeper of the Ground — '

'I am Space Commander Travis, an officer and accredited representative of Earth Federation.' His face behind the partly concealing black mask was assertive, threatening. 'As an agent of my government I demand an immediate explanation of this!'

'Primitive *and* pompous,' Giroc cackled gleefully.

Sinofar looked questioningly at Blake.

'Blake. I'm not a Federation officer . . . but I'd like an explanation, too.'

Travis cut in. 'Blake is an enemy of the state and a fugitive. He is my prisoner,' and took half a pace forward before colliding with a solid yet invisible barrier. He fell back, blinking in surprise, his hands reaching out to gauge the confines of his prison.

Blake cautiously did the same, encountering an invisible yet nonetheless real force field all around him.

Giroc was delighted at the expression on Travis's face. 'Primitive, pompous *and* stupid!' she giggled.

'Giroc!'

'All right, all right,' the old woman whined pettishly. 'It's just that there is such violence in him. He is exciting!' And then, as if ashamed of what she had let slip, 'Old instincts die hard, Sinofar.'

'I know. I know.' Again the same tone of sad resignation.

'You will release me from this force barrier,' Travis demanded, his clenched fists raised threateningly.

'There are things that you must know first,' Sinofar told him softly.

Travis thrust his face at her. 'You do realize that any hostile act against me will be regarded as a hostile act against the Federation. Do you have any idea of the risk you're running?'

Sinofar allowed herself a tolerant smile while Giroc hid her face, highly amused by Travis's crude threats.

'They don't seem very impressed, Travis,' Blake said

mildly, folding his arms. 'Why don't you try stamping your foot?'

'You're very cheerful, Blake,' Travis snarled, fixing him with a cold, merciless eye, 'for a dead man.'

'Do you intend to hold us prisoners?' Blake asked the two women.

'No,' Giroc croaked.

'You were responsible for what happened to my ship?'

'It will be restored when this matter has been settled,' Sinofar assured him, and to Travis, 'as will yours. No harm will come to your crews or your ships.'

Giroc spoke up. 'You have seen what we can do. We are capable of protecting our planet.' She glanced disparagingly at Travis. 'Your threats of reprisal are meaningless.'

'Our powers grew out of a thousand years of war,' Sinofar told them calmly. 'Out of hate and fear and the will to survive . . .'

Giroc took up the story. 'We built destruction. Weapons that your peoples have not yet dreamed of. Every passing year brought new and more powerful ways to kill, and through the centuries the war raged across our planet.'

'With each generation there were fewer of us. The dead vastly outnumbered the living. And still there was no victory for either side.'

'How did it end?' asked Blake quietly.

Giroc leered sourly. 'Another development of another weapon. We demanded their surrender. They refused. The weapon was used. Those that we called our enemy were annihilated.'

'You won,' said Travis stolidly, his face hard and brutal. 'That's what counted.'

But Sinofar shook her head wanly. Her eyes held an infinite reservoir of sadness. 'It wasn't a victory. It was only the end of the war. We were left with a planet made barren by radiation. Our children were monsters, or they died, or were never born.' She looked at the two men. 'This we won.'

74

'How many of you are there now?' Blake asked, concerned.

'We are a dead race,' Giroc replied drably.

Sinofar held out her slender graceful hands. 'We have told you this so you will understand our reasons for intervening in your . . . dispute.'

'Tell us,' Giroc frowned. 'What *is* your dispute?'

Travis jerked his head at Blake. 'I told you — this man is an enemy of the Federation. Tried and condemned. I must bring him to justice or kill him.'

'And you?' Giroc inquired, raising her sparse eyebrows.

'I *am* an enemy of the Federation,' Blake admitted. 'It is corrupt and oppressive. I will destroy it. If I can.'

Sinofar's serenely beautiful face showed no emotion as she contemplated the two men before her. 'Irreconcilable viewpoints,' she pronounced calmly. 'Your differences cannot be resolved without the destruction of the other's belief. The classic pattern for war.'

'I was about to resolve our differences when you interfered,' Travis hissed, fuming with pent-up rage. 'I would have destroyed him and his ship.'

'How many are there in your crew?' Sinofar asked Blake.

On the *Liberator*'s large screen his crew had watched all this in silence. They could see Blake and Travis and the old crone known as Giroc, but not the other speaker, who from the sound of her voice was a young woman. Now Blake was answering her question, looking directly at the screen as if speaking to someone there.

'There are seven of us . . . no, six. Zen doesn't count really.'

'Five,' Avon drawled. 'Neither does Vila.'

'Four,' Vila retorted bitingly. 'Zen's more human than you are.'

Gan pressed his big square hand to his forehead. 'Would almost be worth getting killed to shut you two up,' he sighed wearily.

'Listen!' Jenna hissed angrily. '*Listen!*'

On the screen Giroc was saying, 'And in your ship?'

'Nine,' Travis answered shortly.

Then they heard, but did not see, Sinofar saying, 'Fifteen people could die because of your beliefs.'

'My crew are with me by their own choice,' Blake replied.

'Really?' Avon said in mock surprise, his tone sardonic.

'We can leave whenever we wish,' Cally reminded him defiantly.

Vila made a flapping movement with his hands. 'Would now be too soon?'

Standing near the monument, Travis said brusquely, 'Mine have sworn allegiance to the Federation.'

Giroc nodded her wise old head. 'I'm sure they're all splendidly loyal and dedicated.' Her tone was derisive, taunting him. 'I'm sure that you could both find supporters for your causes and each of you could be backed by a massive army.'

'But would numbers change the nature of the dispute?' Sinofar asked shrewdly.

'Probably not,' Blake conceded.

'Look, what *is* this?' Travis wanted to know, glaring from one to the other. 'Are you preaching pacifism and brotherly love?' He spat the words out with a kind of mocking disgust.

'Of course not,' Giroc answered at once.

'We understand that men will kill for their beliefs,' said Sinofar coolly.

'And that is precisely what we intend to let happen,' added Giroc.

There was an odd, strained silence for a moment, and then Travis said slowly:

'What does that mean?'

'Each of you wishes to destroy the other,' Giroc said in the manner of someone pointing out an obvious fact. 'We are going to give you the chance.'

Blake narrowed his eyes. He said quietly, 'A duel? Is that what you're suggesting?'

'A fight to the death,' bleated the old crone in her thin cracked voice, grinning toothlessly at them both.

'We will ensure that the loser's ship has an opportunity to get away,' said Sinofar, briskly impersonal. 'A limit to the deaths. Don't you find that rational?'

'No,' Travis snapped. 'When I've killed Blake I'll simply hunt down the others!'

'That will be your choice, should you survive,' Sinofar told him indifferently. 'We cannot control your actions beyond this planet. But there will be no destruction, no space wars, within our influence.'

'Aren't you putting artificial limits on your responsibility?' Blake asked, an edge of sarcasm to his voice.

'Responsibility must have limits or it cannot be maintained,' Sinofar replied loftily.

Blake shook his head. 'I don't believe you. Travis is right, you're interrupting a skirmish, not stopping the war. Your "contest" won't solve anything.' He surveyed the two women alertly. 'You must have another reason for this charade. And I don't think I want to kill for your entertainment.'

'You have no choice,' Giroc croaked slyly.

Blake ignored her and looked towards Travis. 'We could agree not to fight.'

'We could,' Travis said neutrally, neither agreeing nor disagreeing.

'*If* you trusted one another . . . .' Giroc smirked, chortling to herself.

'There is another reason.' Sinofar lifted her head. Her eyes were glacial, her voice the merest chill whisper. 'A lesson we would have you learn about death.'

'We both know too much about that already,' Blake said grimly.

'Yes, you know what it is to kill,' Sinofar acknowledged softly. 'But here you must take a life directly. There will be no distance between you and death. No machines to make the act unreal.' She reached out a pale hand, her delicate fingers hovering in the cold night air. 'You will touch the life you take . . . .'

Travis shuffled his feet impatiently. 'Shall we get on with it?'

'There is a door for each of you,' Sinofar intoned. 'Once through that door you cannot return, you must go on.'

'You can return only when it is over,' Giroc added.

'Weapons?' Travis asked.

Sinofar nodded. 'You each have a knife' — and as the words left her mouth two broad-bladed hunting knives appeared on the ground.

Giroc bustled forward, hands clutching the robe to her shrivelled chest. 'As keeper of the Killing Ground I must tell you that there are dangers other than yourselves.' She pointed a crooked finger at the knives. 'These are tools for survival. Do not waste them.'

'How long have we got?' asked Blake, suddenly businesslike, slipping the knife into his belt.

'There is no limit except your physical endurance,' Sinofar told him.

Travis stood arrogantly, hands on hips. 'So this is your "lesson",' he sneered, curling his lip derisively.

Giroc gazed up at him. This time she wasn't smiling. Her face was bleak and pitiless. 'Half the lesson. The death of an enemy. The other half is the death of a friend.'

On board *Liberator* the crew both saw and heard the old woman on the screen, but no one immediately realised the significance of what she had said. They looked at one another, puzzled, rather nervous, and it was Gan who was the first to see what was happening. He lunged towards Jenna, calling out her name frantically, but it was too late.

Even before he had taken two paces she had faded away to nothingness, snatched from their midst in the twinkling of an eye.

As was Android One, the female humanoid machine on the leading pursuit ship.

Two women — one if only technically so — required by the Keeper of the Ground to take part in the oldest ritual of all.

'No! I've had that lesson — I've seen friends die!'

Blake looked desperately from the old woman to the cool and serene Sinofar, but neither one paid any attention to his plea.

Travis was less fussy. 'Nothing concerns me but my duty.' He slid the hunting knife into his belt.

'It begins,' said Sinofar, raising her hands. 'You will each walk forward.'

Travis was looking at Blake. His cruel, swarthy face bore an expression of venomous hatred. 'I don't care about their motives,' he murmured. 'I shall enjoy taking your life.'

'You talk a good fight, Travis.'

Travis took two steps foward and vanished.

'I do care about your motives,' Blake told Sinofar. 'And if any of my friends should die because of you . . . .' He let the threat hang in the air. Then taking two steps forward, he instantly disappeared, as if walking through a door into another stratum of spacetime.

Sinofar's eyes were closed, the lids pressed tightly. Her hands were raised to the starlight, palm upwards, and the disc began to glow with the power of concentrated thought.

Giroc clasped her hands together and her whisper filled the cosmos.

'Now watch . . . and learn.'

6

It was uncanny. In mid-stride Blake had vanished from the desert plain and stepped straight into a forest glade. He spun round, expecting to see the monument and the black cliffs of glass rearing into the darkness, but there were only trees swaying and creaking in a thin, chill breeze. And it was now daylight — he had been mysteriously transported in space and time to a place that had all the illusion of reality. But was it real? The ground was solid enough, and the wind convincingly cold, making him shiver. Blake looked cautiously round, his senses straining. Somebody or something was moving in the undergrowth. Stooping low, he ran silently across the clearing and into the cover of some bushes.

Even stranger was the fact that those on board *Liberator* could see everything that was happening on the screen. They had watched Blake suddenly appear out of nowhere, stand listening for a moment, and then move into cover.

Avon was bemused by it all. 'How can we be seeing this?' he asked, turning with a frown to the others.

Cally supplied the answer. 'We watch through the mind of the one called Sinofar,' she informed him.

'It may be just an illusion,' Avon ventured, observing the screen where Blake was crouching, obviously alert to the approach of someone.

'No.' Cally shook her head slowly. Her telepathic powers told her differently. 'It is happening.'

Blake was in no doubt. The forest was real enough. And someone was moving stealthily through it. Poised and waiting, his hand gripping the knife, he caught a movement as the person came out of the trees and stepped into full view.

Blake rose silently, hefting the knife. 'Jenna!'

She whirled round, startled, and then released a deep sigh of relief. 'That was unkind.'

'How did you get here?'

Jenna shrugged. 'I don't know. But it seems that your weird ladies have picked me to demonstrate the death of a friend.'

Blake stared at her. 'You heard all that?'

'They beamed it to the ship's main screen,' Jenna nodded. 'Everything else is held in some sort of stasis beam.' Her eyes sought his. 'What do we do?'

'Have you seen any sign of Travis?'

'No. I haven't seen any sign of life at all.'

Blake peered round at the trees and the dense undergrowth. 'First thing is to see if we can make some weapons.' He led the way to a thicket and spent several moments selecting a likely-looking branch. 'I don't think Travis will be hard to find. If he runs true to form he'll lay some sort of trap and then try to draw us to it.'

Jenna watched as he trimmed the branch to serve as a stave. 'Who do you suppose he's got with him?'

Blake tested the stave, bracing it against the ground. 'His pilot, maybe?' he grunted. 'Must have given our hosts something of a problem. How do you demonstrate the death of a friend to a man who hasn't got any?'

Jenna flicked back a wisp of hair, pouting slightly. 'I wouldn't be sorry if we didn't mention that part of it any more.'

'I won't let anything happen to you, Jenna.'

'Assuming you have a choice,' she retorted laconically.

Blake grinned at her, then set about sharpening the end of the stave to a point. When he was finished he balanced it in his palm and handed it to her.

'Not exactly a neutron blaster,' Jenna commented, hoisting it. 'Better than nothing, though.'

'Not much better.' Blake wasted no time in seeking another suitable branch.

Travis pointed to a young tree on the edge of the clearing.

'That one.'

The female android went mechanically about her task. There was a splintering crack of timber and she emerged into the clearing with the tree trunk held under one arm, casually tearing off the branches.

'Good. Get me eight more like it.'

Android One dropped the denuded trunk on the ground and turned back.

'And do it quietly.'

'Your opponent is not in the vicinity, sir.'

'I want to keep it that way until we're ready for him.'

Travis moved into the shadow of the undergrowth, examining the ground carefully. He rummaged around with his foot and bent down to grasp the end of a tangle of creepers, pulling out a long green strand which he wound round his hands, testing for strength. Satisfied that it would bear the strain, Travis began to gather more, so involved that he was unaware of a figure standing not ten metres away.

It was the ethereal, ghostlike presence of Sinofar, hardly more than a vague blur of light, observing his every move.

Gan was watching the screen from the Flight Control desk. 'He's definitely working to a plan,' he concluded, glancing to where Vila was vainly attempting to get a spark of life out of the instrumentation display.

'I wish *we* were,' Vila grimaced.

Avon appeared on the Flight Deck. 'Well? Did any of the controls respond?'

Gan shook his head. 'Nothing here.'

'Nor here,' said Vila.

'No,' Cally said from the communications console.

'That's it then. I've done everything I can.' Avon gazed round at the silent banks of instruments and display panels. 'Every machine except life-support is frozen.'

'Even Zen.' Cally gestured to the curved fascia of the ship's master computer — normally alive with a rapidly changing sequence of lights — now ominously blank.

'At least that proves what I've always said,' Avon declared caustically. 'Zen is a machine.'

Vila looked suspiciously at the blank fascia. 'Unless he just doesn't want to get involved.'

Avon's attention had been caught by the activities on the screen. 'What's he doing?'

Cally swung round in the chair, her intense green eyes watching Travis as he knotted several lengths of vine together. 'As Blake said, he is preparing a trap. It could be a mistake. That sort of war is best fought on the move.'

Armed with crude wooden spears, Blake and Jenna were moving stealthily through the forest. The vegetation was a strange hybrid mixture, trees and plants of different climates growing side by side, as if the forest had been artifically constructed: a compilation of specimen flora chosen by a crazy botanist.

It was strangely unreal and yet, perversely, frighteningly lifelike.

'Blake,' Jenna whispered. 'The light's going.'

Pools of shadow were deepening beneath the trees; above the ragged treetops the sky was a dirty opaque yellow, seeming to close in on them as darkness descended.

Blake had halted. He said in a low voice, 'We'd better find somewhere to shelter for the night. I have a feeling this place won't be quite so quiet once it gets dark — '

Even before he had finished speaking an unearthly choking scream reverberated through the forest. Then another, and yet another, from varying directions, so it seemed there were beasts lurking all around. Jenna shivered and pressed closer to Blake's side. She gazed fearfully into the gathering darkness. Blake took hold of her arm and led her forward to a large tree with thick spreading branches. He hoisted her up and began to follow, clambering up to where the branches diverged and formed a natural hollow. They were about fifteen feet from the ground.

Blake settled himself as best he could and looked down. 'Let's hope those things can't climb trees.'

'Or fly,' Jenna shuddered. 'How many hours of darkness do you suppose there are?'

'However many, it's going to seem like a hell of a lot more,' Blake muttered, his face set. 'Look, why don't you try and get some sleep? I'll take the first watch.'

'I couldn't sleep. Not yet. I'll keep watch if you think you can.'

'Actually, I'm sure I can,' Blake yawned, easing himself into a comfortable position. 'Wake me when you get tired, all right?'

Jenna leaned against the trunk, listening to his breathing becoming deeper and longer as he drifted into sleep. She looked out unseeingly into the dark forest, feeling her heart beating hollowly in her chest, and in the distance heard the faint wailing cry of a predatory night creature.

Android One lifted her head at the sound. 'The night hunters are working,' she said dispassionately.

'We'll finish this at first light.' Travis straightened up, casting his eye over the heavy staves lashed together with creeper. He felt supremely confident and smugly pleased with himself. Blake and his companion — he assumed she was female — were in for a nasty surprise come the morning.

Picking up the stave he had fashioned into a crude spear, Travis moved to the nearest large tree, followed obediently by the android. Cupping her hands as a support, she heaved him up into the lower branches, then scrambled up beside him. In the darkness her deathly white face resembled a skull, the eye sockets black and empty.

'I hope Blake has enough sense to do this,' Travis murmured, more to himself than addressing the android. 'I don't want him eaten before I can kill him.'

Finding the most secure and comfortable position, he prepared for sleep.

'Keep watch,' he ordered curtly.

'Yes, Commander.'

Android One, perched precariously on a branch, began the long night vigil.

A gurgling scream shocked her into consciousness. There was a violent thrashing in the undergrowth nearby followed by a terrified gibbering that was cut short as the predator ripped at its victim's throat with tooth and claw. Then in the sudden silence the muted sound of tearing flesh.

Jenna put out her hand to steady herself and nearly fell. She looked round blearily, trying to orient her senses in this strange hostile environment. Guiltily she realized that she had dozed off, sliding imperceptibly into an uneasy half-sleep filled with the grunts and scuffles of the forest.

Blake was still sleeping. She could just make out the pale oval of his face and his outstretched hand, palm upwards, lying on the branch, and something —

Jenna screamed and recoiled. A large black creature with pointed wings, like a bat, was wrapped round his hand, its teeth buried in his wrist.

'Blake!' Jenna screamed.

Blake jerked upright and with a strangled cry of loathing plucked the creature away with his free hand and flung it into the darkness. He shuddered with pain and disgust, holding his wrist tightly.

'Are you all right?' Jenna gasped.

Blake swallowed and found his voice. 'What was it?'

'I fell asleep. I'm sorry. Are you all right?'

'A small cut, that's all,' Blake said, examing the wound. He let go a gust of air.

'I'm sorry,' Jenna murmured, ashamed.

'It's all right, it's all right. My fault. We should have both stayed awake.' He gripped her hand to reassure her, cold and clammy to his touch.

Neither one of them had any further desire for sleep, and with the first faint light of dawn they climbed down stiffly from the tree, thankful that the long night was over.

'It's quite a deep bite,' Jenna said anxiously, looking closely at his wrist. 'Looks inflamed.'

'Made my arm a bit sore,' Blake admitted, opening and closing his hand rather gingerly. He fastened his cuff and picked up the sharpened stave. 'Still, nothing I can't cope with.'

Together they began to move through the trees, fully awake now and alert for the first sniff of danger.

The android was already at work on the framework of wooden spikes when Travis awoke. He jumped to the ground and stretched himself, working his shoulders in the tight black leather tunic to ease the cramp. Around the base of the tree were the scattered corpses of several batlike creatures, their bodies crushed, their wings torn off.

Travis picked one up between thumb and forefinger. 'What are these?'

'They came in the night,' Android One replied blandly, carrying on with her work. 'I trapped them.'

'You did more than trap them.'

'My serum supply is running low,' Android One explained tonelessly. 'There was a little blood in each of them.'

'There was a lot of blood in me.'

'There still is, Commander. You are a Federation officer. As am I.'

'As long as you remember that.'

'Do you now believe we androids are vampires?' It was an academic question, as if she were not really interested in the answer.

'I believe you're useful,' Travis said shortly. 'Let's get on with it.'

She glanced up at him, her face like a death mask. 'My function will be impaired if I do not get further serum soon.'

'Maybe that can be arranged,' replied Travis cryptically.

They worked in silence, each intent on their own task,

Travis strengthening the framework with shorter cross-pieces and binding the whole arrangement securely, the android knotting and weaving strands of creeper into a crude though serviceable rope. When it was finished they stood side by side and surveyed the frame of nine sharpened staves, lying points uppermost on the ground.

Travis brushed his gloved hands together, a slow sly smile forming on his thin lips. He jerked his thumb at the android, and they began to lift the spiked framework off the ground.

The rapt silence on *Liberator*'s Flight Deck was broken by Vila's piping voice. His bright button eyes were fixed on the screen, watching with a puzzled frown as Travis and the android manhandled the frame into a vertical position and hauled it across the clearing.

'Is that what I think it is?'

'I don't imagine it's a recreational aid,' remarked Avon dryly.

Vila looked round at the others, clearly bemused. 'I can't see Blake throwing himself onto it, though, can you?'

'I can't see Blake ever finding the right place,' Avon said, propping his chin on his hand.

'How's he supposed to find it?' Asked Gan.

Cally said, 'He is quartering the area. It is the correct search pattern.'

'If it's the correct area.' Avon's heavily lidded eyes met hers and then resumed their flat indolent stare at the screen. He seemed almost bored.

Travis crouched over a small fire, feeding twigs and leaves into the flames. The clearing was now empty; the lashed frame of spiked staves had been hidden away.

'This will draw Blake to us,' Travis said, glancing over his shoulder at the android. 'Since I was given you, he must have been given a companion also. I want you to find the companion and bring her back here. Dead or alive, it doesn't matter. Just get her,' he finished bluntly.

'And Blake?' Android One queried.

'No!' Travis's eye blazed for a moment. His voice dropped to a vehement whisper. 'Don't touch Blake. He belongs to me.'

Android One turned to go and then hestitated.

'Well — go on. What's the matter with you?'

'The blood of those creatures . . . it was not suitable.'

Travis dismissed her with a wave of his hand. 'There'll be plenty of suitable blood when you've caught Blake's companion.'

Android One nodded and left the clearing. Travis scooped up a handful of damp vegetation and scattered it over the fire. He craned his neck to watch the column of thick smoke rising sluggishly into the still air. It would be visible for miles around.

'They may not even be in this area.'

Blake wiped the sweat from his brow and halted by a small tree. They had covered a lot of ground but had seen and heard nothing.

'We have to assume that they are,' Jenna said, shrugging.

'Maybe I can see something from up there.' Blake grasped the slender trunk, wincing a little. His wrist was sore and his arm had begun to stiffen. He climbed up with difficulty, using his good arm to haul himself into the upper branches.

Jenna held her spear at shoulder height, her eyes probing the bushes. She took a couple of deep breaths to steady her nerves, poised and alert, ready for trouble, and her straining senses picked up a furtive rustling sound from a patch of scrub not five metres away. Turning slowly towards it she held her breath and listened. Nothing there, she decided, relaxing slightly, and turned back. The android was standing beside her. Jenna recoiled with shock, staring into those lifeless eyes, and before she could recover the android chopped savagely down on her neck and caught her before she hit the ground.

Tossing Jenna over her shoulder, Android One moved

stealthily away and disappeared into the trees.

Jenna struggled back to the light, a sickly ache throbbing at the base of her skull. There was a patch of yellow sky, and treetops swaying in the breeze, and somebody moving just beyond her range of vision.

The android looked down at the girl, hands and feet bound with creepers, lying at the base of the tree. The girl's eyes were clouded with pain above the strip of material that effectively gagged her.

Kneeling down, Android One prepared for the transfusion. She was very calm and methodical. First she extended her right hand, palm uppermost, and pressed the button in her forearm. A long hollow needle slid down from the cuff of her tunic, across the heel of her hand, jutting out several inches. Then, quite deliberately, she turned her hand over and brought it down towards Jenna's exposed wrist, the tip of the needle probing for the artery. The girl would supply all the rich fresh blood she required. She found the artery and was about to thrust in the needle when Travis's voice rang out.

'Not yet!'

The android paused. 'I need blood.'

'Not yet,' Travis beckoned to her impatiently. 'Get to your position.' And when she hesitated, he barked, 'Now!'

Android One rose to her feet and moved slowly away, her feet dragging slightly, her face corpselike in the close-fitting helmet.

Travis strode to the edge of the clearing, his back towards Jenna, and called out:

'Blake! Can you hear me?' His face twisted in a sneering grin. 'Yes, of course you can hear me . . . .'

Which was true. Blake was nearer than he thought, crouching in the undergrowth to one side of the clearing, behind Travis and not twenty paces from where Jenna lay. He began to edge forward as Travis boomed out confidently:

'I have your friend. I also have an android which needs blood.'

Blake scanned the clearing, seeking to locate the android. Failing to spot her, he began to creep forward once more, one eye on Travis, who was still looking out into the forest and seemingly unaware of his presence.

'I'm going to let the android have your friend's blood unless you give yourself up . . . .'

Jenna was struggling frantically against the constricting ropes, her mouth working against the gag, her eyes wide and mutely pleading as Blake covered the last few paces and dropped to one knee beside her. She seemed to be trying to warn him of some imminent danger.

Following the direction of Jenna's horrified gaze, Blake looked upwards to where the framework of nine sharpened staves was suspended by the woven creeper in the tree above, creaking gently in the breeze.

With a gloating smile of triumph, Travis spun round.
'Now!'

At Travis's harsh command the android slashed at the woven creeper, but in her weakened condition the blow was neither fast nor strong enough, and she hacked at it again, finally severing the last few strands. The frame of spikes plunged downwards, Blake desperately heaving Jenna's body out of the way and diving after her as the frame crashed to the ground, the sharpened staves burying themselves deeply in the earth.

'Too slow!' Travis yelled at the android in fury, and snatching up his stave he hurled himself across the clearing in a murderous rage. Blake leapt nimbly to his feet to meet the attack, grasping his stave firmly in both hands, and the two of them lunged and slashed at each other, circling, jabbing, parrying, the dust swirling up in a yellow cloud.

Android One at once saw her opportunity. Running to Jenna's side she knelt down and extended the hollow needle from her forearm, the blonde girl writhing helplessly as the android prepared to draw her blood.

Hard pressed as he was, Blake glimpsed what was happening and tried to to go Jenna's aid. But Travis was even quicker to react, and as Blake turned aside he swung his stave in a wide arc, catching him a glancing blow on the side of the head. Blake went down, stunned, and through the pain and the swirling dust saw Travis raise the stave in both hands and drive it downwards with all his might, the point aimed directly at his heart. Grunting with the effort, Blake twisted his body and rolled to one side, the sharpened stave missing him by inches and biting into the soil. Travis wrenched at the stave, attempting to release it, and Blake smashed him across the shins and in the same movement was up and running, wielding the stave like a club.

The needle was at Jenna's wrist, about to be thrust into the artery, when Blake delivered a crushing blow to the android's head, striking her on the front of the helmet and hurling her backwards. He barely had time to cut Jenna's hands free and drop the knife at her feet before Travis was upon him once more, and he met this new attack with the knowledge that the strength in his injured arm was ebbing away with every passing second.

Neither was Android One done for. Climbing groggily to her feet, she stumbled towards Jenna — still bound at the ankles and holding the knife with both hands in front of her. Lunging forward, the android gave a muted plaintive cry as her legs folded under her and she fell on the upturned point of the knife, the broad blade rupturing the serum capsule contained in her chest.

Meanwhile, Blake was fighting a losing battle. His arm was throbbing painfully as again and again he fought off Travis's savage lashing attacks. Realizing he had the upper hand and scenting victory, Travis allowed himself an arrogant smirk of triumph. It was a mistake. Something inside Blake snapped and his face contorted with fury. Smashing through Travis's defences like a madman, impervious to anything except the desire to wipe the smug conceit from his face, Blake drove his adversary backwards with a rain of blows until, overcome by the sheer viciousness of the attack, Travis sagged to the ground, the stave knocked out of his grasp by a final numbing blow.

Standing astride him, Blake thrust the point of the stave

at Travis's offered throat. A terrible consuming rage made his hands tremble as he stared down at the hated face with its single hooded eye and moulded black mask concealing the ravaged features. So easy to kill . . . so easy to snuff out the life of the one man who had sworn he would never rest until Blake was dead. So easy . . . .

With a mingled look of pity and disgust, Blake tossed the stave aside and, without a backward glance, went wearily towards Jenna and held out his hand.

Sinofar stood near the monument, her hands still raised and her closed eyes upturned towards the night sky. Giroc shuffled forward as Blake and Jenna materialized before them. She muttered something under her breath and Sinofar came out of her trance, turning to regard Blake and Jenna almost with hostility.

'You fought well,' Giroc said, though her voice begrudged her words.

'I'm glad you enjoyed it,' Blake said icily. 'I want to go back to my ship now and get under way.'

'We did not enjoy it,' Sinofar said bleakly.

'Neither did we,' Jenna retorted.

The old woman peered up, her wizened face sharp and inquisitive. 'Why didn't you kill him?'

'Too tired. Or too weak . . . .' Blake gave an indifferent shrug. 'Or maybe I just didn't trust your motives. Besides, as long as he's alive he'll be the one chasing me. And I know I can beat him.'

Giroc sniffed. 'At least you're not stupid.'

Blake gestured towards *Liberator*, the brightest star in the sky. 'I need enough time to get my ship away and recharge the energy banks.'

'Your energy banks have been recharged,' Sinofar told him. 'I will see that your ship gets away.' She paused, as if in momentary contemplation, and said thoughtfully, 'Perhaps there was nothing for you to learn.'

'There was something,' Blake corrected her, meeting those serene ageless eyes. 'Another reason why I didn't kill Travis. I would have enjoyed it.'

Liberator was once again in deep space, many parsecs distant from the planet Amersat, barren Memorial to the Dead. All the crew were on the Flight Deck, listening to Blake's account of the duel while Gan tended to his injured arm.

'What was she like?' Gan asked, binding the wound.

'Who?'

'Sinofar.'

'Didn't you see her?' Blake said, glancing round at the others. 'She was very beautiful.'

'All *we* saw was the ugly one,' Vila scowled. 'How is it you get all the fun?'

Blake recalled the events of the last twenty-four hours, culminating in a bloodthirsty android, near death by a frame of sharpened staves, and the ferocious fight with Travis which all but ended in disaster. Not forgetting the bat bite.

'Just lucky, I suppose,' he said with a grin.

Part Two

1

The screen showed a landscape of pure blinding whiteness. At first sight it would have been easy to mistake this for a malfunction in the long-range scanner, though on closer inspection it was possible to make out vague topographical features through a dense snowstorm that blanketed the entire planet. Few forms of life could exist in such extreme conditions — and only then if they were supremely adapted after several millennia of evolutionary trial-and-error or possessed the intelligence to find shelter from the all-pervading arctic cold that held the planet in an icy grip.

Blake's expression was worried and pensive as he turned away from the screen and spoke to the master computer.

'Zen, can you get an estimated surface temperature from this range?'

The bank of lights on the curved fascia flickered in rapid sequence and the calm, unhurried, rather superior voice reported:

'*Sensors indicate a temperature of minus one hundred and eighty degrees and still falling.*'

Vila regarded Blake, poker-faced. 'That's on the cool side,' he suggested. 'If you're going down you'll need thermals.'

Blake nodded briskly. 'Right. Will you see to that?' And as Vila skipped across the Flight Deck, looked towards Cally at the communications console. 'Are you still getting Avalon's signal beam?'

'It's gone on to automatic now,' she advised him, 'and changed position by about eight Earth miles. Static at the moment.'

'Then that will be the homing beacon,' Blake decided, rubbing his chin. 'Lock on to it and get a precise fix.' There was something bothering him . . . an indefinable feeling of foreboding about this planet of ice. Perhaps he was getting jumpy for no good reason. Shrugging off the nagging sense of unease, Blake got on with the task of bringing *Liberator* in from space and positioning her correctly above the planet's snowbound surface.

'Jenna, get your bearings from Cally and take us into a fixed orbit just inside teleport range.'

'That will put us inside the snow belt. The planet has a very deep atmosphere.'

'That's all right. It shouldn't give us any problems.' Blake swung round in the thickly padded command seat, very alert and businesslike now. 'Gan, any space activity?'

'Not any more,' the burly man replied, glancing up from the complex instrumentation display. 'There was a formation of three interceptors patrolling in the sub-atmosphere, but they've moved round to the other side of the planet.'

'Watch for them coming round on the reverse,' Blake ordered curtly. His dark eyes widened a little in alarm as Avon came up with an armful of computer-processed printouts, a dauntingly thick stack of closely tabulated data.

'I've got all the memory bank stuff here. Climatic, geophysical, historical, socio-political profiles. You want to look through it?'

Blake regarded the foot-high batch with a wry grin. 'Looks pretty hefty . . . can you give me a rundown?'

'All right.' Avon settled himself in the adjoining chair and began to reel it off in his precise, clipped manner. 'We've picked a bad time to come. The planet has just entered its winter cycle. They call it the Long Cold, and I'm not surprised. It lasts fifteen Earth years. There's a surface layer of rock and soil, but below that it's permafrost. Solid ice.'

'Any intelligent life?'

Surprisingly, yes. A humanoid creature called a Subterron. They live in the ice caves.'

'Why are the Federation interested in the planet?'

'I was coming to that,' Avon said. 'They annexed it about thirty years ago. It was discovered that mineral deposits that seep down into the ice are subjected to fantastic pressure in the big freeze-up. They're formed into a diamond-like stone of incredible purity — they call them Ice Diamonds. There's nothing else like them in the Universe.'

Blake was intrigued. 'How do they mine them?'

'They use the Subterrons as a slave labour force.' Avon raised an eyebrow, watching Blake shrewdly. 'More important, the Federation uses the Ice Diamonds in the manufacture of light-emitting weapons. Because of their purity they have a greater range and intensity than any other known material. A handful of these must be worth quite a bundle.' He added specualtively, 'Maybe that's what this Avalon character is after . . . .'

Blake's shake of the head was definite, precluding doubt. 'No. It's not for personal gain. There isn't a Federation planet in this system where Avalon hasn't risked death to establish resistance movements.'

Avon's tone was mocking. 'Another do-gooder,' he scoffed.

'Come down with me and find out,' Blake invited. 'Meet Avalon for yourself.'

But Avon was looking at the scanner screen which showed the blizzard raging, unabated. With a slow shake of the head he declined the offer.

'No, thanks. You go ahead and do the heroic stuff, Blake. I'll stay here in the warm.'

And raising his eyes to the screen, Blake couldn't find it in his heart to blame him.

Thick flakes of snow, driven horizontally by the keening wind, battered the rock face and swirled about the entrance to the ice cave where the Subterron stood guard, his heavy coat of shaggy furs almost obliterated by a covering of white. Visibility was down to zero. Adjusting the position of the old-fashioned projectile rifle slung over his shoulder, he stamped a few paces from the cave mouth in an attempt to revive circulation. Inside the fur hood, his face was completely hidden by a close-fitting gauze mask, his eyes protected by dark convex lenses which lent him the appearance of a bulbous-eyed sea creature. Halting by a wall of packed snow, he peered out into the dense white frenzy, seeing nothing, hearing only the moaning shriek of the wind as it swept remorselessly from the Northern polar cap.

Behind him, the smooth wall of snow began to tremble. Slowly it crumbled away and two arms reached out, seeking him. The snow cascaded down to reveal a Federation android clad in a thin one-piece coverall, his face also covered by a gauze mask.

Unsuspecting, the guard stamped his feet in the deep snow, hardly realizing what was happening as two hands clamped his neck in a vicelike grip, and together the android and the guard sank out of sight in the whirling blizzard. There was a faint cry, little more than a whimper, and the android rose to his feet, silent as a wraith, a smear of red on his tight seamless sleeve. Moving to the mouth of the cave, he activated a small round device strapped to his wrist, no bigger than a chronometer — a sonic-line transmitter — and almost at once two androids appeared out of the snow.

Without a further word or sign the three identical figures in the lightweight acrylic coveralls entered the cave mouth, withdrawing from their belts the standard service-issue sidearm, the V-911 para-handgun.

The cavern was spacious, with a high vaulted roof that was lost in shadow; walls of crystalline ice glinted and sparkled in the lamplight. Food stores, bedrolls and other supplies were stacked neatly at intervals, and in a natural niche a sophisticated short-wave communications unit had been set up. A dozen or so Subterrons, hardly distinguishable one from the other in their heavy hooded coats and masks, moved purposefully about the cavern as they attended to their duties. Thus preoccupied, not one of them was prepared for the sight of three Federation androids standing in line abreast, weapons levelled, in the main entrance passage.

Reaction was slow and too late. Giving a warning shout, a Subterron dived for the rack of weapons, his futile attempt coming to grief when one of the androids calmly aimed and fired, the searing blast starkly lighting up the cavern, the Subterron falling to the ground with a bloody gaping hole in his chest.

'Nobody move.'

Even though uttered in the drab toneless voice of an android, the command carried sufficient menace to check any further movement. The Subterrons watched and waited, their expressions completely hidden by the gauze masks.

From out of the dark passage stepped a tall, broad-shouldered figure wearing a heavy, black leather great-coat. Only part of his face was visible in the dim light of the lamps, as if the rest was obscured by something black and shiny. His single eye swept over the silent muffled cave-dwellers.

'Which of you is Avalon?' demanded Space Commander Travis.

Nobody stirred.

Not a patient man, Travis drew his hand weapon, strode up to the nearest Subterron, threw back the fur hood and ripped off the gauze mask. It was evidently not the person he was seeking.

'Don't waste my time,' Travis said in a chill deadly voice, and pressed the muzzle of his gun against the man's temple. 'I want Avalon.'

A moment ticked by. Travis's finger tightened on the trigger-button. Then a figure detached itself from the group and came slowly forward. Thrusting his hostage aside, Travis approached the heavily furred figure, ripped away the hood and tore off the mask to reveal Avalon. Even he seemed taken aback — as much by her youth as her beauty — tousled raven-black hair framing an oval face in which two dark slumbrous eyes blazed defiantly up at him. A face of strength and character and steely determination; remarkable in one so young.

'Who betrayed us?' Avalon said in a low firm voice, held tightly under control. Spots of colour burned in her cheeks.

Travis's reply was a lazy, contemptuous smile. With an abrupt jerk of his head he summoned one of the androids.

'Take her.'

As she was led away, Travis holstered his weapon and turned his attention to the communications equipment. An indicator light was winking on and off to a steady, regular pattern.

'A transmitter?' said one of the androids, standing at his shoulder.

Travis nodded thoughtfully. 'Putting out a homing signal, I imagine.'

The android raised the butt of his handgun, about to smash the equipment, and Travis held up his hand.

'Leave it.' He seemed privately amused by something. 'Let's make it easy for Blake.'

Nodding with quiet satisfaction, he turned on his heel and started for the cavern entrance. The Subterrons waited passively, unarmed and defenceless, and Travis spared them only a brief indifferent glance as he went out.

'Finish it,' he murmured absently, and the cavern was filled with the crackling flare of sustained fire as the two androids diligently and efficiently obeyed the order.

Jenna held the flight controls lightly, her delicate touch manoeuvring the huge vessel into precise coordinated position above the planet's surface. She loved handling the powerful craft in tight orbital situations where her skill and experience as a pilot were put to the most crucial and rigorous test. At such moments, *Liberator* was her baby.

'. . . three . . . two . . . one . . . and holding.' Her eyes darted like quicksilver over the instrument displays housed in the flight console. 'Cut in auto orbital drift compensators.'

'Compensators in,' Gan responded crisply.

'Gravitational negators in,' Jenna ordered.

'Grav negs in.'

'Confirm position and status,' Jenna said to the master computer.

'All systems confirm instrument readings. Our status is firm.'

Jenna released the controls and leaned back with a sense of accomplishment and pride. 'That's not bad. We've flown seven-and-a-half million miles and brought her in right on the button.'

'Nice going,' Blake congratulated her.

Zen's sequence of lights changed and steadied.

'The navigation computer registers a positional error of point oh-oh-oh-oh-oh one of one degree. Automatics are compensating.'

Jenna glared at the curved fascia. 'You computers certainly know how to shatter a girl's ego.'

'He's just jealous because you can do it as well as he,' Blake grinned. He swung round. 'Avon, have you got the teleport coordinates?'

'All set.'

'All right. Let's go.'

Along with Avon and Cally he set off for the teleport section, pausing at the exit port to issue final instructions to Jenna and Gan:

'Keep the sensors on full alert. Those pursuit ships might still be in the area.'

'We'll watch for them,' Gan promised.

'Good luck,' called Jenna brightly.

'Thanks.'

Preparations were well under way in the teleport section. Avon and Vila were at the control desk checking the coordinates while Cally strapped on her belt and sidearm, making sure the power unit was fully charged. Both she and Blake wore lightweight thermal suits with a thermostat dial incorporated into the front left shoulder. Taking five teleport bracelets from the rack, Blake slipped one on his wrist and zipped the rest into his arm pouch.

'We've got a blizzard at surface level,' Vila reported in a matter-of-fact tone, 'and the temperature is down to minus two hundred.'

'Set your suit temperature to mark eleven,' Blake told the girl, adjusting the dial on his own suit.

Cally did so and reacted as the heat enveloped her in a suffocating cocoon. 'Wow,' she gasped, wriggling uncomfortably.

'Stay at the controls,' Blake said to Avon. 'If it goes right we'll be back up in fifteen minutes.'

'We'll be ready and waiting,' Avon confirmed.

'Bring me back an Ice Diamond,' Vila quipped, grinning cheekily.

Cally was standing in the transmission area, curly spirals of hair clinging damply to her flushed face. 'Hurry it up, will you, or I'm going to be fried before we get down there . . . .'

Blake joined her and gave the signal. He saw Avon's hand operating the slide control and at once the teleport section shimmered and faded — and without any appreciable sensation he was immediately surrounded by a swirling maelstrom of whiteness and buffeted head-on by a freezing wind that sounded in his ears like a banshee's mournful wail.

Cally staggered back from the force of the impact and turned up the heating dial another couple of notches. She tried to speak but the words were whipped out of her mouth and lost in the raging blizzard. Struggling forward, she stumbled over something and went down on her knees, and as Blake reached out a hand to assist her they both saw the humped shape thickly covered with snow. It was the body of the guard. Brushing the snow from the masked face, it took Blake only a moment to ascertain that he was dead, and with a grim look at Cally he rose to his feet and drew his sidearm. Cally did the same.

Pressed close together, they sought the shelter of the cave mouth, pausing warily for a moment before advancing along the descending passage. The sight that met their eyes made them halt in stunned horror.

The heat blast from the energy weapons had partially thawed the cavern walls so that the bodies of the dead Subterrons were encased in icy tombs, the sub-zero temperature having rapidly re-frozen the melted ice. The dim lamplight shone eerily over the hunched bodies, fixed in grotesque glassy attitudes of death.

Blake moved cautiously forward, brushing a thin film of water from the surface ice. 'The attack must have been in the last hour or so. It hasn't quite re-frozen.'

'What do you think happened?' Cally whispered numbly, her green eyes still mirroring the shock of the dreadful carnage.

Blake gazed round bleakly. 'My guess is that Federation Security found this place . . . there was a fight and — '

'There couldn't have been,' Cally objected. 'None of these people are armed.' She pointed to the rack of weapons, now covered in a thick layer of ice. 'The weapons are still in the racks.'

'The heat blast from the guns must have melted the walls and floor,' Blake decided. 'Now it's freezing up again.'

'They couldn't have stood a chance.' Cally turned away, fighting to keep control. 'Let's get out of here, Blake.'

'Not yet. I've got to know if Avalon is amongst them.'

'I don't want to see any more.'

But there was a job to do and Blake had to finish it. 'Cally, you've met Avalon,' he told her bluntly. 'You're the only one who can identify her. We've got to know for certain. Now, come on . . . . '

Bracing herself, Cally turned back and began to examine the corpses in their coffins of ice, peering at them closely and then moving on with a brief shake of her head. Blake had spotted the short-wave transmitter and he stepped across to it, seeing the steadily winking light inside the thick cascade of ice which now enclosed the equipment.

'The homing beacon is still transmitting. Federation Security must have located the frequency, and once they'd picked it up they wouldn't have had any trouble finding this place.'

Cally had moved deeper into the cavern to a point where a natural buttress shielded a recess from view of the main entrance. As she straightened up, having failed to identify another of the dead Subterrons, her eye fell on something which made her react with an urgent cry.

'Blake!'

It was the feebly moving form of a man, the lower half of his body locked in the ice, and Blake went swiftly to his side and removed the fur hood and mask. He was in his twenties, with fair hair and a fresh open countenance, and as Blake felt for his pulse the man's eyelids stirred, and he uttered a low moan.

'He's alive, all right. Let's get him free of the ice.' Blake moved slightly to one side. 'Use your handgun. Lowest setting.'

Cally drew her sidearm linked by the coiled wire to the power unit in her belt, and set the dial to minimum. Holding the barrel close to the ice she carefully loosed off a short blast, and as the ice cracked and crumbled Blake pulled the young man clear and propped him in a sitting position.

'Is he all right?' Cally asked, holstering her weapon.

'I think so.' Blake brushed his hand across the man's shoulder and the fur powdered away in tiny fragments of cinder. 'He must have been on the fringe of the blast. The furs are scorched right across his shoulder.'

The young man came suddenly awake and tried to struggle free, his hands pawing the air, his light blue eyes hazy and alarmed.

'It's all right, it's all right,' Blake calmed him. 'Take it easy.'

The blue eyes hardened into focus and swept round the cavern. 'The others . . . ' he managed to say hoarsely. 'What about the others?'

Blake shook his head gravely. 'As far as we know

you're the only survivor.'

'What about Avalon?' Cally asked, kneeling beside him. 'Was she here when they made the attack?'

It took the young man several moments to remember. He gazed around aimlessly and said haltingly, 'She was with us . . . she . . . they took her out . . . . ' Then it flooded back and his voice took on a new strident note.

'They took her away before the firing started . . . . Avalon's a prisoner!'

The central area of the medical laboratory was brightly illuminated by four large reflector lamps set at an angle in the low soundproofed ceiling. On every wall except one, banks of electronic equipment, alive and humming, needles quivering in their dials, were ranged on metal racks, and in place of the fourth wall a single sheet of tinted plate-glass separated a smaller room from the main area.

Within the harsh circle of light, strapped to an inclined board and wearing a hospital-type smock, Avalon was undergoing a meticulous examination by two white-coated scientists. Their interest, it seemed, was purely objective; they might have been compiling physiological data on a new humanoid species, noting every detail and recording their observations on clipboards. While one examined her eyes, nostrils and mouth — and even clipped a small piece of hair which he placed in a test tube — the other was taking precise caliper measurements of her hands, fingers, feet and toes. They worked with an air of quiet methodical calm, totally uninterested in the girl as anything but an object of scientific curiosity.

In the penumbra of shadow outside the bright focal point of light, Travis stood indolently with arms folded, watching with little more than passing interest. Nearby, the austere ghostly presence of an android merged with the background of complex electronic equipment, having as much affinity with the machines as it did with the humans present.

Responding automatically to the discreet beeping

107

sound from the wall communicator, the android listened attentively, replaced the handset, and moved deferentially to Travis's side.

'The Supreme Commander's ship has landed, sir. They've already disembarked.'

'Good. I think we're just about ready.' Travis was about to dismiss the android when he had another thought. 'Oh, I'll need a human to assist in a test. Check the Detention Block. See if they can give you someone.'

'Any special characteristics?'

Travis gazed into the cone of light, his voice flat and indifferent. 'No, an unskilled low social grade will do. An expendable.'

'Very good, sir. I'll see what I can find.' The android turned stiffly about-face and left the laboratory.

'Any problems?' Travis inquired pleasantly, coming to stand at the lower base of the inclined board. His eye roamed over the girl's body shrouded in the shapeless smock. He might have been observing a waxwork doll.

'Not that I can see.' The older of the two scientists, a corpulent man with thinning grey hair, slipped the calipers into his pocket and made a note on his clipboard. 'A good healthy specimen. No deformities or unusual features. The standard triple-omega should provide a perfect basis.'

'Then the work can be completed quickly?'

The man nodded and cleared his throat. 'I should think so. We have a very experienced team standing by.' He smiled briefly. 'Everything is ready.'

'Good . . . .' Travis tapped his gloved thumb against his chin. He held up his forefinger. 'And remember, if you hit any snags — if there's any extra specialized equipment you need — you have an absolute priority rating.' His voice became suddenly harsh and grating. 'Demand anything you want on my authority.'

The scientist nodded appreciatively and raised his eyebrows at his colleague. With such high calibre authority behind them the experiment was bound to succeed.

Avalon had listened to all this with a certain stoic defiance. Now Travis folded his arms and looked directly into her grey-blue eyes, the thick black lashes in striking contrast to the pallor of her youthful, almost demure face with its fine bone structure.

He spoke gently, with a trace of condescension, as if to a child who'd been promised a birthday treat. 'You should be flattered than we consider you important enough for all this special attention.'

'Anyone who opposes the Federation knows what to expect if they are captured. It's a risk we're all willing to take.' It was a more a factual statement than an opinion, demanding nothing, giving nothing away.

'That's obvious, Travis agreed smoothly. 'And frankly, I wish I could find the same degree of dedication and sacrifice in the people who serve me. But then, my people don't have a "cause" do they?' He sneered the word at her.

'Every year more and more of them openly defy the Federation. In the last century more than thirty planets have seceded from union with the Federation. Others will follow.' Her eyes watched him unflinchingly. 'Many others.'

Travis nodded, pursing his lips. 'Well, you'll tell us about those very shortly. Their locations. Their leaders. Their plans. I'm sure we'll be able to convince them that they are making an error.'

Avalon smiled thinly. 'I know enough about your interrogation machines to realize that I will be unable to resist telling you everything I know. And with that information you'll wipe out hundreds of people . . . destroy underground organizations.' Her voice sank to a whisper. 'But you won't end the opposition. You'll never end it.'

'You're probably right.' Travis seemed unperturbed at the prospect. He went on mildly, 'But we'll just keep on trying. As you say, you will reveal everything we want to know . . . only that can come later.' His single dark eye bored into her. 'To begin with we need you for a much more important venture. You are vital to it . . . so vital we've even codenamed it *Project Avalon*.'

The girl swallowed and moistened her pale lips. She fought back her fear and spat at him, 'Whatever it is, you can't force me to cooperate. I won't help you – '

'But you *are* helping me,' Travis contradicted her silkily. 'At this very moment you're helping me. Simply by being here you have set in motion a chain of events that have been absolutely predetermined.'

He was smiling openly, enjoying the mingled look of confusion and trepidation that was imprinted on her young face.

'I don't understand,' Avalon said, the breath shuddering in her chest. 'I don't know what you're talking about.'

Travis shook his head pityingly. 'Do you think your capture at this particular time was a matter of pure chance . . . mere luck? Not at all. It was a carefully calculated part of my strategy.' He leaned forward so that his face loomed over her, lost in black shadow from the blaze of light above. Very slowly and precisely he said, 'You are worth more to me than an entire fleet of space cruisers. You are going to give me Blake.'

Avalon gazed up at the black silhouette of his head, her blue-grey eyes wide and fearful.

'Blake . . . his crew . . . and most important of all . . . his undamaged ship,' Travis crooned rapturously. 'You're giving me the *Liberator*!'

2

The young man had recovered from his ordeal. His name, they discovered, was Del Chenver, and he had been a member of Avalon's resistance movement from the very beginning. Now it was vitally important, Blake felt, to get every last scrap of information if they were to succeed in mounting a rescue operation, and with this in mind he questioned Del urgently, aware that every passing moment was precious. Avalon's life — or death — hung literally in the balance.

'You're certain that Avalon would have been taken to the city?'

Del nodded. 'Federation Security abandons all the outer fortifications once the Long Cold starts. Anyway, the main interrogation laboratories are in the city — they must have taken her there.'

'All right. It seems reasonable to assume that's where they're holding her.' Blake mulled this over, studying the fair-haired young man. He decided he could trust him; Del Chenver had a look of single-minded fervour tempered with cool common sense that Blake respected. 'Next question: have you ever been inside the city?'

'Yes, I worked inside for a time in one of the labour gangs. We were all restricted to the lower levels, though, so I don't really know my way around too well.'

'Do you think you could get us in?' Cally asked.

Del stared at her, aghast at the idea. 'Go into the city? You can't do that!'

'Listen,' Blake ground out in a low voice. 'Avalon knows more than any other one person about the resistance movements in this star system. Names, places, everything — '

'She won't tell them anything,' Del said loyally.

'I don't doubt her courage, but with the questioning techniques they use now they can probe straight into her memory. In a couple of days they'll know everything she knows.'

Cally joined in. 'It will be a tremendous setback,' she informed the young man gravely. 'Even worse, a lot of people will be eliminated. We must get to her before that happens.'

Del bit his lip, his pale blue eyes clouded with uncertainty. He began to see that they were right, that their options were reduced to this one slim chance. He said tentatively, 'We'd never make it through any of the normal entrances, they're all identity-linked and manned by android guards.'

'What about ventilation shafts?' Blake asked.

'No, not a chance. In the Long Cold they're closed off and the atmosphere is recycled.' Del shook his head, thinking hard. 'Wait a minute, though . . . . The regeneration plant is outside the city. It's linked by inlet and outlet ducts.' His eyes brightened as the possibility took shape. 'We might — we just might be able to get in that way.'

Blake's jaw was set. 'Then we'll have to try it.'

'Now hold on,' Del protested, worried about what they might be letting themselves in for. 'There's no guarantee it'll work. They're bound to have all kinds of security devices built into the system.'

But Blake wasn't as naive, nor as rash, as Del had supposed. 'We've got an expert on that kind of thing,' he said, exchanging an amused look with Cally, and brought the wrist communicator close to his mouth. 'Blake. Do you read?'

Jenna answered at once, waiting alertly on the Flight Deck for his call.

'Jenna. We hear you.'

'We're going to need some help.' Blake's voice issued hollowly through the speaker. 'Tell Vila to put on a thermal suit and get down here.'

Vila leapt up like a scalded cat, his eyes wide with panic. 'Why me?' he yelped. 'Oh, now wait a minute. It's cold down there, and I'm a temperate climate man. I don't function well in anything under sixty-five degrees.'

'You're wasting time,' came the sharp response. 'Get down here and bring your bag of tricks.'

Vila glowered at the speaker grille and slouched towards the exit port. 'I don't know why it always has to be me,' he muttered to himself. 'Any little problem comes up, it's always me . . . .'

'Any space activity?' Blake inquired.

Gan spoke up. 'A ship came in and docked at the city base about half an hour ago.'

'Could you identify it?'

'The detectors read it as a Federation Command vessel. The angle of orbital approach suggested it could have come from Federation H Q.'

Blake was disturbed by this news. He looked worriedly at Cally and Del. 'Might be something to do with Avalon's capture,' he surmised. 'Maybe they're planning to ship her out of here.'

Cally read the implication at once. 'Then we'll have to move quickly,' she declared firmly.

Blake nodded and spoke into his communicator. 'Come on, Vila, hurry it up. Over and out.'

Which was precisely what Vila was trying to do. When Jenna arrived in the teleport section he was zipping himself into a thermal suit, all fingers and thumbs with nervousness, and still muttering under his breath.

Jenna handed a slip of paper to Avon with the teleport coordinates. 'That's the location based on the voice fix.'

'Right.' Avon moved the two variable transparent markers across the digital grid, pinpointing Blake's exact position. He glanced up expectantly. 'You all set?'

Vila clipped on his teleport bracelet and picked up the hold-all containing his unauthorized entry equipment. 'Wait a minute,' he said, fumbling with the thermostat dial in his suit. 'I want to set this to maximum.'

Avon breathed an impatient sigh and Jenna stood

nearby, hands on hips. Vila twiddled the dial and let out a shriek of anguish, as if he'd been plunged in boiling oil, his face flushing bright scarlet.

'Turn it down, you idiot!' Jenna called out.

'Not me,' said Vila obstinately. 'If it comes to a choice I'd rather fry than freeze.' He stepped into the transmission area, running a finger round the sealed collar of the suit and blowing out his rosy cheeks. 'All right, put me down before I turn into one massive blister.'

Avon operated the controls and Vila dematerialized, finding himself a split second later in the gloomy ice cavern, staring into the face of an ice-bound corpse. He gulped and averted his eyes, looking round fearfully before seeing Blake and stumbling thankfully towards him.

'Now, what's the problem?' he asked churlishly.

Blake gestured towards Del Chenver and quickly introduced the two men. 'Avalon's been taken prisoner,' he went on, wasting no time. 'We're going to try and get into the city to free her.'

Vila greeted this information with a marked lack of enthusiasm, glancing reproachfully at Del Chenver.

'Come on, we'll get started,' Blake said crisply. 'Del, you lead off.'

The fair-haired young man led the way towards the entrance passage, Blake behind him with Cally and Vila bringing up the rear. Vila was trembling noticeably.

'You're not cold, are you?' Cally asked, concerned.

Vila nodded dismally. 'It's not the temperature,' he explained, slithering after her over the frozen cavern floor. 'Just the icy chill of fear.'

It didn't comfort him when all she did was grin.

'We're all finished. Got everything we need.' The scientist with the thinning grey hair made a final note on his clipboard and slipped his stylus into the breast pocket of his white coat. He regarded Travis with the hint of a satisfied smile on his fleshy features.

'Very well. Take her down to Transfer. They're standing by.'

The two scientists raised the inclined board on its wheeled trolley and prepared to move it from the laboratory. Avalon's face was impassive, her dark eyes fixed unblinkingly on the ceiling. Travis turned away and motioned to the android who had returned with a small, underfed, grey-faced individual clad in a dirty brown one-piece prison uniform. The man blinked myopically around him at the brightly lit clinical laboratory, obviously on edge and fighting hard to control his shaking hands.

The android indicated the prisoner with a jerk of his head.

'Will he do?'

Travis looked him over indifferently. 'Yes, he seems healthy enough,' he decided. 'He should do quite well — '

The heavy metal door of the laboratory suddenly slid back on its oiled track and a tall android in an immaculate full dress black uniform, helmet gleaming and with a handgun in a burnished holster at his hip, marched in five regulation paces, surveyed the room, and nodded briskly to someone in the corridor.

The faintest trace of expensive perfume preceded Servalan as she swept in, rivetting the attention of everyone. Her trim diminutive figure was swathed in black furs, her perfectly proportioned head swaying above the lavish open collar like a slender, graceful flower. As always, Travis was struck by her poise and quite breathtaking beauty. He stiffened a barely perceptible fraction, inclining his head towards her.

'It's good to see you, Supreme Commander. You had a safe journey, I trust?'

'Nothing is safe any more.' Servalan regarded him coolly and went on as if she were discussing the weather. 'You've heard, of course, that there have been two more attempts to assassinate me . . . .'

'Yes.' Travis nodded solicitously. 'I was most concerned.'

'I can't go anywhere now without this wretched bodyguard,' Servalan complained, glancing with distaste

115

to where the tall, impressive android stood at attention, one hand resting alertly on the butt of his para-handgun. 'The Administration insist he is with me at all times.'

She began to peel off her black furs, draping them at arm's length without even bothering to look, the android bodyguard taking each piece as it was casually discarded. Underneath the furs she was attired in a crisp all-white uniform that was tailored snugly to the nearest millimetre. Ignoring everyone else in the room, and speaking to Travis as if he were the only person present, she continued imperiously:

'I blame Blake for it. Not directly, of course, but news of his activities is getting around. The people seem excited, they sense something. The fact that he's still free gives them hope. It's dangerous, Travis . . . hope . . . the expectancy of something glimpsed and desired. Very dangerous.'

Travis watched her carefully. 'I think we can be fairly confident that the source of that hope will be soon eliminated,' he promised.

'It's essential that it is.' Servalan spoke without fear of contradiction. 'I think it's only fair that you should know that there has been considerable criticism of your handling of the Blake affair. Your operation has been costly in personnel and resources, and there have been no worthwhile results to justify it.'

Travis's colour rose and his single eye burned with resentment. 'That's not entirely just. There have been two occasions when I could have destroyed Blake – it was only the Administration's insistence that the *Liberator* be captured undamaged that stopped me – '

'In your defence I have made that clear,' Servalan interrupted him smoothly. Her voice adopted a harder, more imperative tone. 'But I can't go on making excuses. I have been under pressure to replace you. So far I have been able to resist that pressure. Now I need your reassurance that my confidence has not been misplaced.'

Travis said smugly, 'I think *Project Avalon* will silence the critics.'

116

'It is an excellent plan,' Servalan agreed, smiling faintly. 'It has every chance of success.'

'I'm glad you approve.'

Servalan raised her finely arched eyebrows and said rather mockingly, 'You should know better than that, Travis. In politics one must never go on record as *approving* anything . . . at least, not until the matter is an undisputed success. However, off the record . . . ' her voice assumed a confidential tone ' . . . you have my full support.'

'Thank you.'

Servalan glanced lazily towards the wheeled trolley, as if noticing it for the first time. 'And this is the famous Avalon, is it?' she inquired, moving closer to where she could observe the girl's supine figure. She clicked her tongue disparagingly. 'I'd expected something more impressive.'

'All the checks have been completed,' Travis informed the Supreme Commander. 'They're ready to take her down to Transfer.'

'Don't let me delay it. Carry on.'

The two scientists nodded deferentially and wheeled the girl from the room. Servalan confronted Travis once again, her manner changing abruptly to one of brisk efficiency. From her belt pouch she took out a small, polished metal container with a hinged lid, raised the two sturdy clasps, and carefully opened it to reveal two clear glass phials nestling in moulded sponge.

'The labs have come up with what you wanted, I think.' Servalan held the container firmly with both hands. 'It's totally new. And very costly.'

'This is the only element that was missing,' Travis gloated, his gloved hand removing one of the phials with the utmost delicacy, as if it were a piece of fine porcelain. 'Now I am almost ready.'

'Good. When will you test it?'

'Immediately. Everything is prepared.' Travis was like a child with a new expensive toy. He went quickly to the console in front of the wall of tinted glass and pressed a series of switches. The small inner room was flooded with light, revealing three bare white ceramic walls, a completely sterile environment in which the only feature was a segmented metal arm with a clawlike device protruding from a sealed aperture.

'I shall be fascinated to see it work for myself,' Servalan murmured, her cool blue-grey eyes following the preparations.

Travis entered the room through a heavy door beside the glass wall and inserted the phial with great care between the jaws of the rubber-covered clamp. Adjusting a calibrated setting so that it was held delicately yet securely, he satisfied himself that everything was in order before returning to the control console. At his nod the android escorted the prisoner into the room and came out, closing the door. Travis threw a switch and there was the sighing hiss of compressed air followed by a dull hollow clunk from the door. At the sound the prisoner started and gazed round, his thin, pallid face harshly illuminated by the overhead lights, obviously perplexed, not knowing what was expected of him.

'Check door seals,' Travis rapped.

The android tried the handle of the door with his full weight. 'Door firm,' he acknowledged.

'Are you ready?' Travis asked the Supreme Commander.

'Whenever you like.'

Looking intently through the glass wall, Travis pressed a button on the panel and they heard the subdued whine of servo-operated hydraulics. At first nothing appeared to be happening. But then — with the slightest of movements — the clamp slowly tightened, everyone watching with fascination as the phial shattered under the vicelike pressure. Immediately the light inside the room took on a bluish hue, as if something had been released into the atmosphere.

Glancing down for a fleeting moment, Travis activated a timing device on the panel, then snapped his attention back to the man in the room.

The prisoner was gazing placidly into space, apparently unaffected by the contents of the phial. Absently, he brushed the back of one hand, as if shooing away a fly, and after a second or two repeated the gesture with growing irritation. It was only when he looked down that he realized, with mounting horror, what was happening to him. Something was growing on his hand. It was like a fungus, grey and cellular and spongelike, and it was dividing and multiplying itself with astonishing, frightening speed. The man began to claw at it desperately, his face stricken with terror, but now it had enveloped both hands and was creeping rapidly up his arms. And as he twisted aside, in wild-eyed panic, the watchers saw that the grey cellular fungus had attached itself to his neck and was devouring his face.

Travis was hypnotized by the sight, tense with excitement, his gloved hands curled into fists; Servalan watched dispassionately, betraying no emotion whatsoever.

The growth had now totally engulfed the upper part of the prisoner's body and more than half of his head. The process seemed to be speeding up by the second. Falling to his knees, the man opened his mouth in a scream of anguish, though not a sound escaped from the sealed soundproofed room. Within moments the struggling mound of grey sponge had lost all resemblance to a human being, not a single feature visible, and after a few slight spasmodic twitches lay completely still, a dead and lifeless mass of fungus.

Gradually the blue glow faded and the room was once again bathed in clinical white light. Travis punched the button on the timing device.

'Forty-three seconds.'

'Very impressive,' Servalan said quietly.

'How long before it neutralizes?'

'It's clear now. Open the door.'

Travis's hand hovered hesitantly over the control, then decisively flipped up the switch. Moving to the door, Servalan waited for the hiss of compressed air to subside before opening the door and stepping inside. Travis

followed, and together they stood looking down at the
inert mass of dead fungus. There wasn't even any smell.
Travis touched it with his foot and the whole thing crumbled away, leaving a small pile of grey dust.

Servalan's lips curved up in a little half-smile.

'Satisfied?'

Travis breathed out slowly, turning to meet her eyes.

'Completely.'

The large pipe was almost buried in the snow, and even
when they had cleared most of it away there was a thick
sheath of ice that had to be melted, enabling Vila to get at
the inspection trap. Blake, Cally and Del were crouched
in a small semi-circle, trying to shield Vila from the onslaught of the bitterly cold blizzard as he worked with
numbed fingers, trying to remove the metal plate.

His face screwed up against the driving wind and snow,
Vila shouted something, but the words were snatched
from his mouth and he had to repeat them through cup-
ped hands.

'It's freezing over again. Give it another blast.'

Cally nodded her understanding and levelled her handgun at the trap. There was a brief flare of energy and the
melted water ran down. Vila gave the thumbs-up and
went back to work.

'He's got all the bolts free,' Del yelled in Blake's ear.
'Why doesn't he pull it clear?'

'It's certain to be linked to a security device.
Unauthorized opening would set off the alarms.'

Cally was staring off into the blizzard, her keen senses
alerted by something. Grabbing Blake by the arm, she
pointed beyond the curve of the pipe to the beam of a
searchlight that was slowly approaching through the
whirling snow.

'Blake! Look!'

'Security robot,' Blake rasped grimly. 'Everybody down.
Get down and don't make a sound.'

The four of them huddled in the shelter of the pipe,
hugging it closely as the security robot trundled up on its

spiked snow track to within a few feet on the other side of the pipe. The beam of the searchlight mounted in the circular dome swept over them, scanning the area; and seeing nothing with its probing eye the robot switched the light off.

They waited, praying that it would now go on its way, but the robot remained motionless, pinning them down. Crouching in the lee of the pipe, Blake cursed between clenched teeth, fretting at their helplessness and at the vital seconds ticking away.

On board *Liberator* the seconds were also ticking away too slowly. It was Gan's turn on watch, but he had stared at the empty scanner screen until his eyelids began to droop with boredom and he had slipped into a quiet doze. Neither Jenna nor Avon thought to check the screen, so when the three tiny pinpoints of light appeared in the extreme corner not one of them noticed. It wasn't till Zen flickered into life and the bland mechanical voice echoed across the Flight Deck that anyone was alerted.

'*Sensors report alien spacecraft entering our ambit.*'

Automatically three pairs of eyes went up to the screen, Gan's blinking sleepily and then guiltily open wide.

'There they are!' Avon said tersely, pointing.

Jenna turned on Gan. 'You were supposed to keep watch!' she flashed angrily.

'I'm sorry,' Gan mumbled, shamefaced. 'I wasn't paying attention.'

'Can you identify them?' Avon asked the master computer.

'*Analysis confirms they are Mark 1V Federation Interceptors.*'

Jenna's face was drawn, her eyes bright and hard as she watched the screen. 'Compute their course, speed and range.'

'*Interceptors are heading towards our position on a direct bearing,*' Zen reported imperturbably. '*Speed: time distort three. Range: two million spacial miles.*'

'Have they seen us?' Jenna asked.

'*Hull sensors register scanning beams,*' Zen confirmed.

121

'They know we're here all right,' Avon declared, making a sour expression. 'What's more, we'll be in their attack range pretty soon.'

Jenna was out of her seat before he'd finished speaking, diving for the communications console. 'We've got to let Blake know.' She began punching the teleport call button frantically.

The security robot hadn't moved, and it crossed Blake's mind that perhaps it had stalled. He looked at his companions helplessly, seeing three humped shapes shrouded in white as the heavy snow settled on them. At least, he reflected, it was camouflage of a sort.

Then without any warning the robot started to move. Its dome traversed at right angles, and they heard the rattle of the spiked track as the robot continued on its way. Blake cautiously lifted his head, breathing a deep sigh of relief, and in that same instant the communicator on his wrist gave out a high-pitched beeping. Ducking back down, Blake clamped his hand over it, trying to muffle the piercing sound.

The robot had halted. The searchlight came on and swivelled towards them in a wide arc. As if having second thoughts, the robot reversed in its tracks, taking up the same position as before. Huddled against the pipe, Blake and the others remained as still and silent as marble statues.

'He's not answering!' Jenna called out, her voice strident with alarm and frustration. She jabbed the button repeatedly. Still nothing.

Gan tore his eyes away from the screen. 'They're coming in very fast. What do we do?'

'Only one thing we can do — run for it,' Avon said flatly. 'We can't chance a fight with three of them.'

'If we go out of teleport range Blake will be stuck down there!' Jenna told him fiercely. 'When the time comes he'll need to get out fast!'

'And if we stay here there won't be any ship left to come up to. Our only hope is to make a fast orbital flight and try and lose them — if we do that we can move back onto station.'

Jenna and Gan exchanged uncertain looks, still reluctant to make a decision, and Avon snapped at them:

'Well? Have you got any better ideas?'

They evidently hadn't, judging from their expressions.

'All right, then, let's get out of here. Take her on manual, Jenna.'

As the girl moved swiftly to the flight control position, Gan said morosely, 'I just hope he's not in any trouble down there . . . .'

Blake was simply thankful that his communicator had stopped its tell-tale bleeping. And he was even more thankful when, after a prolonged survey of the area, the security robot decided to move on. This time they waited until it was safely out of range before emerging from the cover of the pipe and shaking off the snow.

'All right,' Blake said doggedly, brushing the thick layer of snow from the inspection trap. 'Let's get on with this.'

Once again Vila went to work.

'Yes?' The android listened for a moment. 'Very well. Understood.' He replaced the handset on the wall communicator and crossed the laboratory to where Travis and Servalan were seated at a desk.

'Space Security report that our interceptors have made scan contact with an alien ship.'

'Has it been identified?' Travis asked, sitting forward.

'Available data indicate that it could be the *Liberator*.'

'Could be?' Travis uttered a gruff chuckle of delight, beaming all over his swarthy face. 'It is! I'll stake my life on it! What action has been taken?'

'Our interceptors are in pursuit.'

'Shouldn't you call them off?' Servalan inquired, frowning.

'No need. They can't match *Liberator*'s speed,' Travis informed her. He added shrewdly, 'And it would look unnatural if they didn't take some action.'

'Quite right,' Servalan nodded. 'It mustn't appear too easy.'

Travis rose jubilantly to his feet, filled with confidence, smacking his left fist into his gloved palm. 'If I read my man correctly we can expect him to try and enter the city within the next twelve hours,' he prophesied.

'Then we must make sure that everything is ready,' Servalan murmured with a sly, sideways smile, rising to join him. 'Shall we check?'

Travis stood politely to one side and followed the Supreme Commander to the door. *Project Avalon* was going precisely according to plan. His plan.

The highly polished interior of the pipe gleamed in the light of the torch beams. There was a constant flow of air in the same direction as they were walking, and up ahead — not far away from the sound — the throbbing whine of powerful suction fans.

Blake halted by a meshed inspection plate in the curved wall of the pipe and the others crowded up to him.

'Shall we try this or move on further?' he asked Del.

The young man looked into the darkness beyond while he considered. 'I calculate we should be well inside the city now,' he decided. 'Let's chance it.'

Blake nodded and beckoned Vila forward. 'You're back in business.'

Kneeling by the inspection plate, Vila gave it a quick professional examination, then jutted out his lower lip dubiously. 'This is fastened by double-headed Kleiber bolts on the other side,' he advised them. 'You'd need half a ton of explosives or a genius to open this.'

'We don't have any explosives,' Blake said dourly.

'Then it's lucky I'm a genius,' Vila grinned at him, opening his bag of tricks. 'Watch this.'

The cell door stood open, flanked on either side by an armed guard. After a moment the two scientists emerged into the corridor, closing the door firmly, and from the pocket of his white coat the older man took a small embossed plastic card which he inserted into the electronic lock. There was a faint buzzing sound followed by a distinct click, and the man returned the card to his pocket.

Several other doors, all with the same locking device, lined the narrow corridor, and beside each one, set into the wall, a closed-circuit TV monitor with a control unit.

Moving off, the two scientists encountered Travis and Servalan, who had just appeared round the corner.

'You've finished with her?' Travis inquired of the older man.

The scientist nodded, evidently well pleased. 'We've just put her in the cell.'

'Was everything satisfactory?' Servalan asked, watching him closely.

'Perfect.'

With a curt nod of dismissal, Servalan swept forward to the guarded door and stood with folded arms while Travis pressed the switch on the TV monitor. The picture steadied, showing a small bare cubicle with Avalon sitting on a chair in the corner. Her own clothing had been returned to her, a simple one-piece uniform and knee-high leather boots trimmed with fur. She was gazing straight ahead at the wall, her expression blank, almost docile. She didn't stir all the time they were observing her.

Travis turned off the picture, meeting Servalan's eye with a grin, and spoke to one of the guards. 'You've drawn your issue of new weapons from the armourer?'

'Yes sir,' The guard held out the snub-nosed weapon for Travis's inspection. He checked it briefly and handed it back.

'Stay alert.'

'Sir.'

Taking their time, content in the knowledge that everything was prepared and waiting, Travis and Servalan returned to the laboratory.

The inspection cover moved fractionally to one side and an eye squinted nervously through the slit. A moment later the cover was silently removed and Vila's head peered out cautiously, looking to left and right along the dimly lit concrete corridor. The pipe was high up near the ceiling, a short steel ladder leading up to a platform which gave access to the hatch.

'All clear, 'Vila reported in a tremulous whisper, stepping down onto the platform. Blake and the others swiftly followed, making no sound as they dropped to the floor.

'Do you recognize the area?' Blake asked Del.

'No. Probably one of the sub-levels,' the young man replied, 'but I don't know which.'

'Then let's find out.'

Leading the way, Blake moved furtively along, keeping close to the wall. Turning a corner he came to an unmarked cross junction, four identical corridors stretching gloomily away, and with a sinking feeling realized that finding Avalon in this anonymous maze wasn't going to be easy.

The party pressed on, moving stealthily through the underground levels of the city, watching alertly for any sign that would give them their bearings. At one point they came to an iron staircase leading upwards, and ascended to the next level only to find it exactly like the one they had just left. Blake was becoming impatient with this lack of positive progress. At this rate they could spend days wandering at random through the labyrinth of sub-levels, for all they knew getting further away instead of nearer to where Avalon was being held.

About to turn a corner, Blake spotted a guard in the distance and pulled back sharply out of sight. Drawing the others near, he said in a low, urgent voice:

'We could search this place for ever and not find what we're looking for.' A wicked glint of daring appeared in his dark eyes.' 'I'm going to get us a guided tour.' And even while they were glancing at one another in a puzzled fashion, he went on, 'Vila, you come with me.'

Too surprised to object, Vila tagged along behind as Blake boldly turned the corner and, in full view of the guard, marched confidently forward. The guard looked up alertly at their approach, raising his gun, and was about to challenge them when Blake's voice rang out in a bark of authority.

'You there! What are you doing in this section?'

The guard stared at them through his tinted visor, his attitude at once unsure and on the defensive. 'I was posted here by the Security Commander.'

Blake and Vila were rapidly closing the distance; they had to reach him before his suspicion overcame his cautious uncertainty.

'Damn it!' Blake growled irritably. 'My orders were that no one below middle echelon was to be allowed in this area. What's your Security Commander's name?' he demanded harshly, confronting the guard, feet braced apart, hands on hips.

Vila had edged to one side, slightly behind the guard's left shoulder.

'Sub-Major Carven,' the guard answered meekly, then seemed to regain a little composure. 'Could I have your name and authority, sir?'

'His name is Blake,' Vila told him genially, pressing the muzzle of his handgun into the guard's neck. 'And this is his authority.'

The guard froze and made no attempt to resist when Blake relieved him of his weapon. Blake shouldered it and said in a crisp, no nonsense tone:

'You have a woman prisoner here called Avalon. Where is she being held?'

The guard's Adam's apple moved up and down in a dry gulp. 'All prisoners are kept in the main Detection Block.'

'Then take us there . . . now.'

The guard stared at him, stubbornly refusing to move, and Vila prodded his neck with the gun.

'The man said *now*!'

Pushing him in front, they set off along the corridor. Vila glanced behind, giving a low whistle, and Cally and Del hurried along to join them.

Blake flattened his shoulders to the wall and risked a look into the corridor where the two guards stood flanking the door to the cell. He eased back out of sight and turned to the guard, still under Vila's watchful eye.

'You're sure that's it?'

The guard nodded sullenly.

"All right.' Blake slipped his handgun into the holster and held up a warning finger under the man's nose. 'Now you do exactly what I told you — and remember, there are going to be two guns right behind you all the time.'

The guard licked his lips and swallowed.

'Then let's go.'

Side by side, Blake and Vila marched into the corridor, the guard a few paces behind as though escorting them. As they approached the cell door, one of the guards on duty unslung his weapon and held it in both hands as if to bar their way.

'Halt!'

The guard escorting the 'prisoners' cleared his throat and said with a nervous croak, 'I have two prisoners who are to be confined in Detection Room 4.'

'This area is under maximum security and totally off limits,' he was informed brusquely. The two guards exchanged glances, obviously suspicious, and came forward.

'I have written authority,' the other guard said unconvincingly, and began searching his pockets as through to find the relevant document. Then his nerve went completely, and bending double he dashed between Blake and Vila, yelling in a voice shrill with panic:

'Get him! It's Blake!'

There was a split second's indecision before his words sank in, and both Blake and Vila used it to full advantage. Leaping forward, Blake caught one of the guards in the solar plexus and followed up with a short vicious jab to the heart that sent him sprawling. He collided with the wall and went down heavily. Vila hadn't been so fortunate. He was still engaged in a fierce tussle with the other man when Cally and Del raced forward to assist him.

But Blake was alive to another threat. The guard who had escorted them was running towards the far end of the corridor for all he was worth. If he managed to raise the alarm they were done for. Grabbing Cally's arm, he thrust

128

her through the mêlée of bodies with a terse, 'Get after him!'

With Del's help the other guard had at last been over-powered, Vila finishing the job with the butt of his hand-gun, knocking him out cold.

'We've got to move fast,' Blake urged them. 'They're going to be swarming all over us in a minute — '

He stabbed the button on the TV monitor and the picture blinked on showing Avalon, alerted by the scuffle, staring at the door.

Blake tried the door and, seeing the electronic locking device, called Vila forward. 'Get it open, quick as you can.' Stepping aside to allow Vila to work on it, he stared at the screen, then turned to Del.

'That *is* Avalon, isn't it?'

'Yes,' the young man nodded. 'And they don't seem to have harmed her.'

Cally appeared at the end of the corridor and ran to join them. 'I lost him,' she reported breathlessly. 'He got into a transit shaft.'

Somewhere near at hand in the underground complex the blare of a security alarm shattered the silence, to be almost instantly reinforced by several more, coming from every direction.

'That does it!' Blake said grimly. 'Check your teleport bracelets. Cally, cover that end.' As the girl sped off he took a bracelet from his arm pouch and handed it to Del. 'Put that on and then get down and cover that end of the corridor.'

The young man looked puzzled for a moment, then clipped the bracelet on, scooped up a weapon that had belonged to one of the unconscious guards, and did as he was ordered.

Blake opened the voice channel on his bracelet and spoke into it. 'Stand by on teleport. We're going to need to come up fast. Confirm.' There was no answer. Anxiously, he thumbed the button again. '*Liberator* . . . . Confirm! Do you read me? Come in, *Liberator* . . . .'

There was a sudden crackling burst of fire as Cally held

off a squad of Federation guards, followed almost immediately by a barrage of energy bolts that flared brightly around her. Time was running out.

Vila had at last mastered the locking device. With a final flourish he activated the manual control and the door swung open. Blake stepped past him and entered the cell. The girl's face showed a confused mixture of bewilderment and alarm.

'I'm Blake. I'd hoped we could get you out without quite so much fuss, but we've hit a few snags.' Without further explanation he took her by the arm and led her into the corridor, calling out to Del, 'How is it at that end?'

'Still clear.'

'Right . . . . Vila, Avalon, get down there and wait for us.'

As they went off, Blake tried again to establish contact with the ship.

'*Liberator*, do you read me? Come in!'

Nothing.

With a snarl of annoyance, Blake charged forward to give Cally support. Crouching beside her, he loosed off a sustained hail of fire, and in the brief respite rapped out tersely, 'Get down there with the others. I'll cover.'

Blake held the position until he was sure that Cally had made it to the other end of the corridor. He needed five seconds to get clear before the guards realized what was happening and attacked in force. Spraying a continuous barrage of fire, he whipped round and raced to join the others, not noticing that one of the guards had regained consciousness and was fumbling to train his weapon on the running figure. The first Blake knew of it was when he was hit in the shoulder and sent spinning violently against the wall, the breath buffeting out of his lungs in an agonized gasp of pain.

From a kneeling position, Cally fired a short burst which finished the guard, and was on her feet and lunging to Blake's aid in the same swift movement. She grasped his arm, hauling him upright, and half dragging, half supporting him she got him to the corner and out of the firing line.

Blake, his face chalk-white and running with sweat, was holding his left shoulder. He nodded weakly, holding himself upright, and said through pale lips, 'I'm all right. It's okay. Vila, try the ship . . . . '

Vila spoke urgently into his wrist communicator as Cally and Del held the corner against the guards, who were now advancing slowly along the corridor. There was still no response, however, and Vila looked hopelessly at Blake.

'Nothing at all!'

Blake gritted his teeth. 'There's only one thing for it. We'll have to go out the way we came in.'

And in the next instant the five of them were running for their lives, the Federation guards hard on their heels.

3

Vila was the first of the party to reach the metal ladder
leading up to the small platform. Leaping onto it, he
reached down to help Avalon, and as he did so a guard
appeared at the far end of the corridor and fired a random shot which hit her in the legs. She buckled at the
knees and would have fallen if Del hadn't supported her,
and with Vila's help managed to get her on the platform
and through the inspection hatch.

Blake and Cally gave what covering fire they could, and
then it was their turn up the ladder and through the hatch,
Blake slamming the cover shut behind him and stumbling
after the others down the dark echoing pipe.

The journey back seemed to go on for ever. Twice Vila
thought they had overshot the outer inspection trap, and it
was with immense relief when they finally reached it, tum-
bling out into the freezing night air, the blizzard still
raging as relentlessly as before.

Blake was the last to emerge, hearing the clatter of
boots as the pursuing guards headed along the pipe, less
than minutes away. Avalon was shivering uncontrollably,
her one-piece uniform offering only scanty protection
against the bitterly cold wind and whirling snow.

'What do we do now?' Vila wanted to know, turning his
thermostat dial to maximum.

'She can't survive in this temperature,' Blake insisted,
indicating Avalon who lay huddled between Cally and
Del. 'We've got to find cover.'

'There are some old mine shafts about a mile from
here,' Del muttered, pointing into the blinding
snowstorm. 'That way.'

'Let's try for it,' Blake said grimly, aware that they had

no other option. Bending into the wind, he began to lead the way from the comparative shelter of the pipe, and had gone no more than a couple of metres when the beam of a searchlight stabbed through the darkness, catching him in its full glare. He scrambled back frantically as the security robot loomed out of the surrounding wall of white, firing a jet of flame towards them.

The inspection cover was thrust aside by gloved hands and the Federation guards began to pile out. Vila and Cally got the first two in a rapid burst of crossfire, doing just enough to keep the rest inside the pipe, but with the security robot bearing down on them Blake knew with absolute certainty that the situation was hopeless. They were pinned down, with minimal cover, and had seconds at the most.

In one last desperate, futile attempt, he raised the wrist communicator to his lips, knowing that it was all over.

The murmuring throb of the hyper-propulsion power unit faded away, and in the ensuing silence the Flight Deck seemed charged with high voltage tension. Across the curved fascia of the master computer a new configuration of indicator lights flashed and steadied, and the toneless voice reported:

'*We have resumed original position and status.*'

Jenna heaved a huge sigh of relief and said at once, 'Link in Surface-Space speech channel.'

Everyone stared at the receiver grille as Blake's voice burst through the brief crackle of static. It sounded like the hoarse cry of a drowning man.

' . . . *Liberator*! We need teleport now! Come in, *Liberator* . . . .'

Blake held the communicator close to his mouth, repeating his urgent plea into what seemed a desolate void. The security robot came on, its searchlight blinding them, and from the inspection trap poured a squad of Federation guards, weapons raised and ready to fire. Blake saw the glint of their visors through the snow . . . and then, in the blink of an eyelid, Gan's anxious face

133

staring into his.

'What went wrong?' the big man demanded, running forward into the transmission area.

'Just about everything,' Blake answered shortly. There was no time for lengthy explanations. Avalon looked in bad shape, supported by Del and Vila, and Blake was concerned for her welfare. 'Get her down to a stateroom and take care of her,' he ordered, already on his way to the Flight Deck. 'Let's get this ship moving. If they locate us they're going to throw everything they've got at us. Move!'

Everybody moved.

Avalon's face was a pale mask, almost ghostlike, as she lay back against the banked pillows. Cally sat beside the bed, watching over her, and Jenna stood near Del's chair, her face showing concern.

Cally brushed a stray lock of black hair from the girl's smooth forehead, and as she did so Avalon stirred and tried to sit up.

'You just rest,' Cally soothed her. 'You're safe now.'

'How are you feeling?' Jenna asked, coming to the foot of the bed.

'I'm perfectly all right.' Avalon smiled wanly, then looked down at herself, realizing she was in a nightgown. 'I'd like to get dressed. Where are my clothes?'

'They should be dried out by now,' Jenna said. 'Or I can get you something else to wear if you like?'

'I'd feel more comfortable with my own things.'

Jenna smiled. 'I'll get them for you.' She left the room.

'You just relax for a while,' Cally murmured, tucking the sheets in as the girl lay back. 'We'll all have plenty of time to talk and make plans.'

Del hadn't once moved or uttered a sound. He was gripping the arms of the chair, his eyes fixed unwaveringly on the girl in the bed. The expression on his face, had Cally been able to see it, was tense and full of barely contained menace.

Blake hefted the snub-nosed Federation weapon in both hands and leaned back in the padded chair, studying it thoughtfully. It was the one Del had taken from the fallen guard in the corridor. He checked the firing mechanism, shaking his head in a slow, puzzled fashion.

'I thought I'd just let you know that Avalon is fine,' Jenna said brightly, appearing on the Flight Deck. She held up a bundle of clothing. 'She wants to get dressed.'

'Good,' Blake nodded abstractedly. 'Who's with her?'

'Cally.' Jenna started to leave and then paused, noticing Blake's air of absorption. 'What is it?'

Blake was looking at the weapon and frowning. 'I don't know . . . something is wrong.'

'What do you mean?' Jenna asked, moving towards him.

'I'm not sure. I can't quite nail it down,' he confessed. 'But there's something about our escape that bothers me . . . .'

'Like what?'

'To begin with, the very fact that we *did* escape.' Blake glanced up at her with narrowed eyes. 'Federation troops are highly trained and efficient. They were on their own ground and totally outnumbered us. In spite of that we got out.'

'It was your turn to be lucky.'

Blake gave her a grudging smile. 'If it was, we certainly used up more than our fair share. And we were lucky right from the word go. We found Del alive, he led us directly to the pipeline, we got into the city without too much trouble. We wandered around for quite a while before we located Avalon, but never once did we set off the alarm circuits. Our problems only started once we'd got her out of the cell, and even then . . . .'

Something else occurred to him, and he tapped his left shoulder.

'Look at that. Do you see any sign of damage?'

Jenna leaned forward and then shook her head. 'Seems all right.'

Blake regarded her keenly. 'One of the guards got a clear shot at me. The impact knocked me over. My shoulder is bruised, but that's all.'

'So what?' Jenna shrugged.

Blake held up the gun for her to see. 'These Federation weapons are neutron powered. The hit should have ripped me apart. Avalon was hit in the legs, but she was able to stand and walk before we got back to the ship — '

Rising abruptly, he slipped off the safety catch and aimed the weapon at a metal clipboard lying propped on the communications console. 'Let's try something,' he muttered, and in front of Jenna's astonished gaze fired a short flaring burst that blew the clipboard halfway across the Flight Deck.

Avon and Gan, who had been tinkering with some equipment, leapt out of their chairs and rushed forward, watching with baffled expressions as Blake recovered the clipboard and held it out.

'It's had a nasty kick, but that's about all. No radiation or flare damage.' He tossed the Federation weapon to Avon. 'Take a look at that.'

After a quick expert examination, Avon pronounced succinctly, 'It's not neutronic. Low energy bolt discharge. It could stun or bruise, but it's not capable of inflicting serious injury.'

Gan's broad face creased in bewilderment. 'That doesn't make sense . . . .'

'It would if they wanted us to get away,' Blake said quietly.

There was an absolute dead silence during which everyone stared at him as if he'd lost control of his mental faculties. Then Avon smiled dismissively and shook his head.

'It's an interesting idea, Blake, but hardly logical. The Federation has chased you half across the Universe with the simple aim of destroying you. The one time when they've got you pinned down they let you go.' He raised his eyebrows sardonically. 'No, it just won't work.'

But Jenna had begun to have doubts. 'I agree they could have got Blake,' she said pensively, thinking it through. 'Cally and Vila, too. But there'd still be three of us left . . .

and *Liberator* . . . . '

The light of understanding snapped on in Blake's eyes. It was like a revelation from on high. 'Of course! You're right Jenna — they want the *Liberator* too! And this is the only way they could do it. They have to put somebody on board. It was all set up, and we've fallen for it beautifully.'

'Avalon?' Gan queried.

'No, it can't be,' Jenna objected. 'Cally's met her before. She knows her.'

'Then it's got to be Del,' Avon said.

'But how is he going to do it?' Blake wondered. His tone sharpened as he faced the three of them decisively. 'We've got to find out. Gan, look after things here — and stay alert. You two, come with me.'

They hurried down to the stateroom and came upon a situation that confirmed their suspicions: Cally lying unconscious on the floor, a nasty purplish bruise on her forehead. Del was nowhere to be seen.

'She's going to be all right,' Avon said, checking her heartbeat. 'Help me get her on the bed.'

When she was comfortable, Blake whirled round on Jenna. 'Warn the others. Start a search. He has to be found!'

Jenna dashed out and Blake followed, halting at the door. 'Will she be all right?' he asked Avon.

'I think so.'

'Stay with her.'

Moments later he was running along the corridor and almost ran full tilt into Vila hurrying the opposite way.

'Listen, we've — ' Blake began.

'I know. Jenna told me. Where do we start?'

'Let's try the starboard quarters,' Blake said, not breaking his stride. Vila turned about and followed him at a brisk trot.

Gan looked up, his face wreathed in a pleasant smile as Avalon entered the Flight Deck. 'How are you feeling? Better?'

'I'm all right now, thank you.' Avalon glanced round uncertainly. She was wearing a quilted robe over her nightgown.

'Come over here and sit down,' Gan invited her, extending his hand.

'Where's Blake?'

'He went to look for Del — ' Gan frowned and rubbed his chin. 'But I thought Del was with you?'

'You haven't heard?' Avalon said, her dark eyes watching him closely.

'No. What?'

'He attacked Cally. Then he dragged me out. I thought he was going to use me as a hostage, but then he just let me go and went off somewhere.'

'Then Blake was right.' Gan smiled at her reassuringly. 'Don't worry, they'll find him. Again he noticed her looking round, as if searching for something. 'Is there anything you want?'

'Yes . . . yes, there is. My uniform. There are some things in it I need.'

'I'll see if I can find if for you,' Gan said, patting her on the shoulder, and began looking for Avalon's uniform. He recalled vaguely that Jenna had been carrying some clothing . . . .

Jenna was checking the sleeping quarters, moving cautiously along the corridor and peering into each room. So far there had been no sign of him. She gripped the small locking wheel in the door and slowly turned it, pushing the door open while keeping well clear in case he was lurking just inside, ready to pounce.

Her full attention engaged, she failed to hear the soft footfall directly behind her, and as she backed out of the room, satisfied that it was empty, a hand fell heavily on her shoulder. Spinning round, she stared up in horror as Del's smeared and bloody face loomed over her. His eyes rolled up into his head and with a dull groan he lurched forward and collapsed at her feet.

Controlling the fierce pounding of panic fear, Jenna knelt down, seeing his pale lips trembling as he tried to speak. He was near death. She leaned closer, trying to distinguish the mumbled words through his faint tremulous breathing as the life ebbed out of him.

Gan had found Avalon's clothing. He picked it up and carried it across to her. 'I knew it was around here somewhere.'

Avalon thanked him and swiftly delved into the small bundle, locating the belt and pouch. She unzipped it and took out the small metal container with the hinged lid. Raising the clasps, she lifted the lid to reveal the remaining glass phial in its bed of moulded sponge.

'Hold her!!'

Gan swung round, wide-eyed, at Jenna's shrill warning cry. She was standing in the entrance, arm outstretched, pointing.

'That's not Avalon!!'

Reacting quickly for such a big man, Gan reached out to seize the girl and was hit with such force by her small knotted fist that he was sent crashing back, dazed and winded. It was as if he had been struck by a mechanical pile-driver. Jenna launched herself forward and was thrown aside, of no more consequence than a rag doll.

As Avalon crouched down, prepared to meet Gan's next attack, the metal container fell from the chair, dislodging the glass phial which rolled across the floor.

Before she could retrieve it, Gan was closing in on her again. He circled warily, choosing his moment, but as he went in Avalon met him with a stunning blow that stopped the big man in his tracks. His strength against hers was like that of a puny weakling. The phial had rolled into an open space, and with two strides Avalon reached it and raised her foot to stamp down. Throwing herself headlong, Jenna knocked the girl off-balance, the two of them crashing to the floor in a tangle of arms and legs.

Blake and Vila came onto the Flight Deck at the run, and with Gan's help they succeeded in pinning the girl down, though it took all their combined strength to hold her.

'Get something to tie her,' Blake ordered, both his hands gripping Avalon's slender right wrist. Her power was inhuman.

Jenna straightened up wearily and was about to take a step backwards when Blake's harsh shout froze her to the spot. Peering over her shoulder, Jenna saw the glass phial directly behind her, inches away from the heel of her boot. With bated breath she turned and picked it up, holding it securely in both hands. Only then did she dare breathe out.

The phial was resting in a transparent diagnostic container linked to the master computer. Everyone looked up as the indicator lights adopted a new configuration and Zen delivered his verdict:

'*Analysis indicates the phial contains a parasitic virus of a mutant strain. Fungal in nature, it has a short life-cycle and is self-eliminating.*'

There was a sombre silence as they all reflected on how close they had been to total annihilation. Gan spoke up, voicing their thoughts in his patient, placid voice.

'If she'd been able to break it, we'd have been wiped out. And the ship would have been totally unharmed.'

'It very nearly worked, too,' Avon added gravely, looking down at the motionless form of Avalon on the bench top. He had removed a small plate from the side of the thermoplastic face to reveal a maze of tightly packed solid-state circuitry. He went on with a touch of grudging admiration, 'They made a perfect replica. The best piece of robotic engineering I've ever seen.'

'I still can't believe it,' Cally frowned, staring at the absolutely life-like figure. She raised her bandaged head to look at Avon. 'I *talked* to her . . . we talked about the time we met before. How could a robot do that?'

'They would have done psych-transfers and personality grafts from the real Avalon.'

'But why did she turn on Del?' Vila wanted to know. 'Why kill him?'

Jenna has the answer to that. 'He'd been working for the Federation all along. He infiltrated Avalon's group and found their hide-out. He was planted there after the massacre to lead you into the city, but it was never intended that he should be brought back up to the ship.' She grinned sourly. 'Just his hard luck that you "rescued" him.'

Blake went on, 'When he realized he was going to die along with us, he tried to stop Aval — I mean the robot. It had to kill him then in order to accomplish its mission.' He looked across to where Avon was still working on the robot's internal circuitry. 'Can you make it safe?'

'I can certainly de-programme it,' Avon asserted. 'Scramble its electronic brain.'

'Could you re-programme it?'

Avon shook his head doubtfully. 'Not really. A few basic functions, maybe, but not much else.'

Blake came to a decision. 'Fly on manual, Jenna. Take us back to the same orbital position as before.'

'Go back?' Jenna exclaimed, sharing the incredulous reaction of everyone else.

'That's right.' Blake remained cool and composed. 'Then I want a precise fix for teleport that will put us down inside the city.'

'You're going into the city?' Gan protested.

Blake looked at him with apparent surprise. 'Can you think of another way to get Avalon out of there?'

Travis closed the door firmly, activated the electronic locking device and turned to Servalan with a broad confident smile. Together they sauntered along the corridor of the Detention Block, smug in the knowledge that the plan had worked to perfection.

'I think I'll stay on during Avalon's interrogation,' Servalan mused. 'I have the feeling she will tell us a great deal.'

'I'm sure she will,' Travis agreed.

'When will you begin?'

'I want to finish this *Liberator* business first. We'll get started as soon as it's confirmed we've put across a boarding party. Our robot should have released the virus by now.'

The micro-paging unit in his breast pocket emitted its discreet call signal, and switching it off he excused himself and stepped across to a nearby wall communicator. His dark swarthy face crinkled with growing puzzlement as he listened.

'You're sure of that?' Travis said sharply. 'Keep checking. I'm coming up.' He replaced the handset and turned to face Servalan's questioning look. 'I don't understand it . . . . Space Track Control say that the *Liberator* has moved back into our ambit. It's orbiting over the city.'

'That's not possible,' Servalan said at once. 'It must be another ship.'

'They seem very certain — '

He broke off as the wailing blare of the security alarm system filled the corridor, and turning back was about to reach angrily for the wall communicator again when an android guard appeared and hurried forward.

'What is it?' Travis barked. 'What's going on?'

Even though the android's voice was toneless, it still managed to communicate an underlying note of real distress.

'It's Blake, sir! He's here! In the main laboratory — '

'What!' Travis yelled, his jaw hanging open. 'How . . . ?'

'He's demanding to see you.'

Servalan drew herself up, her eyes like blue chips of ice. '*He* . . . is . . . *demanding*?' she gasped, outraged.

The android became a trifle more circumspect. 'I'm merely reporting what I have been told, Supreme Commander. He also says you are to bring Avalon with you.'

Travis waved the android brusquely away. 'I'll deal with this . . . ' and snapped his gloved fingers as an afterthought occurred to him. 'Bring the prisoner,' he instructed, and set off for the main laboratory with Servalan close behind.

Blake, it seemed, couldn't have been more casual or unconcerned. He stood in the middle of the laboratory with arms folded, his handgun holstered, looking for all the

142

world like someone whiling away the time as he waited patiently for a friend to turn up. By his side stood the immobile figure of the female robot, eyes locked in its sockets, arms held stiffly as if arrested in mid-motion.

The ring of guards, weapons levelled uneasily at Blake, parted as Travis and Servalan entered the room. The two of them came forward a few paces and halted, staring at him with a kind of fervid incredulity.

Blake's eyes were filled with sardonic amusement. 'It didn't work, Travis,' he said lightly. 'It was brilliant, but it didn't work.'

'How did you stop it?' Travis rasped bleakly.

'It's not important now. All I want to do is finish what I started.' Blake's eyes hardened. 'I'm taking Avalon out of here.'

'I don't think so, Blake,' Travis murmured craftily, raising his hand with the three lensed rings. 'You've overstretched your luck this time . . . .'

'That wouldn't be a good idea,' Blake replied evenly, casually pointing to the glass phial which was resting under the toe of his boot.

Servalan's eyes widened with horrified alarm, and she pressed Travis's arm down to his side.

'He wouldn't do it,' Travis grated.

'You have to be very, very sure,' replied Blake softly.

'You'd die, too — '

'Along with you, the Supreme Commander, and everybody else in the city. You want to take that chance?'

It seemed, for just a moment, that Travis was prepared to risk it. His hatred and frustration boiled up inside and his arm lifted as of its own volition, his face contorted with the burning desire for revenge, whatever the cost. But Servalan wasn't willing to sacrifice herself for the cause . . . not even the Federation's.

'What is it you want?' she snapped.

'Avalon.'

Servalan spoke over her shoulder. 'Bring the prisoner in.'

The android escorted Avalon into the room. Her face

was pale and exhausted; she seemed very near collapse.

Travis said stonily, 'You still have to get her out of here. Is your teleport fast enough to stop me killing you both?'

Blake ignored him. He beckoned to Avalon, and she came to stand beside the robot, the exact replica of herself.

'Take the bracelet off its wrist and put it on,' Blake ordered, and waited until she had done so. Then, not taking his eyes from Travis's face, he slowly bent down and picked up the phial, holding it between thumb and forefinger.

'We had to re-programme your machine slightly,' Blake said, still watching Travis like a hawk. 'It's not nearly as sophisticated as it was, but it can perform a few simple functions.' And as if to demonstrate, he said, 'Raise your left hand.'

The arm moved jerkily upwards and stopped.

'Close your thumb and forefinger.'

The robot obeyed.

'Open them a little.'

Blake slipped the phial between them so that it was delicately held, almost balancing between the robot's fingertips.

'I think that's about all,' Blake said smoothly, and spoke into his wrist communicator. 'Stand by to teleport.' Then, facing Travis he explained, 'The robot will crush the phial is response to a trigger word that only I know. So you'd better be very careful what you say.'

With a final mocking smile, he held the communicator to his mouth. 'Bring us up, Jenna.'

Almost instantly Blake and Avalon dematerialized, leaving the room as silent as a tomb. Travis edged forward, the sweat standing out on his forehead, and with infinite care reached at full stretch for the phial. His hand was within inches when it slithered from the robot's fingers and dropped towards the floor. With an anguished shriek, Travis dived with outstretched hand and caught the phial in his gloved palm just as it was about to shatter.

Weak and trembling with relief, he heard brisk angry footsteps as Servalan stalked from the room.

Travis stared straight ahead, his single eye glazed and unseeing. A terrible, all-consuming rage filled his head to bursting point. 'I'll get you, Blake.' The words ached in his throat. 'If it takes all my life, I'll get you!'

4

The two-seater flight compartment of the Spacemaster Series 5 was small and cramped, most of the available room taken up by instrumentation displays, control equipment, forward vision panels and scanner screens. It often occurred to Ensor, the pilot, that the designer had crammed everything in and then hastily remembered at the last minute that the craft was supposed to be manned by a crew of two. It was certainly true that anyone suffering from claustrophobia couldn't have withstood even a short training flight under such conditions, much less lasted out the weeks this particular trip had taken.

Ensor leaned forward to plot the astro-navigational coordinates and, having satisfied himself they were correct, glanced across at his companion. Maryatt was in his late twenties — a good ten years younger than Ensor — with a lean face, prominent jawline, and bright, intelligent eyes. His dark-grey Federation uniform, crumpled after so long in close confinement, bore the triangular shoulder flash of a Senior Medic.

'Take a look out of your port light,' Ensor suggested, easing himself back in the contoured seat. As usual his long legs prevented him from achieving any real comfort.

Maryatt pressed the control and a small panel in the bulkhead beside him slid back to reveal a circular port. He leaned towards it, shielding his eyes against the brilliant light of a vast red orb that completely filled that portion of space.

'What is it?'

'The planet Cephlon. It means we're right on course and time. Just six more space days and we'll have reached our destination.'

Maryatt glanced over his shoulder. 'You keep calling it "our destination",' he said with a trace of irritability. 'Just where is it? What's its name?'

'You'll know, all in good time,' Ensor replied imperturbably.

'But why the secrecy? We're on our way now. There's nothing to lose by telling me where we're heading.'

'Security has become a habit with us. It's second nature. Because of it we've had over thirty years of complete independence. And that is something we value above all else.'

The young medic shrugged and looked once again at the vast red planet. 'Anything down there?' he asked uninterestedly.

'There was once. It was the trading and cultural centre for this whole star system. Very important.' Ensor clicked his tongue. 'Not any more, though.'

'What happened?'

'Global war. Reversion to primitive. Nobody seems sure if there's any life left there. At one time — '

Ensor cut off in mid thought and scanned the instrument panel, his brow furrowing with sudden concern.

'What is it? What's the matter?'

'We're getting trajectory drift,' Ensor said worriedly, speaking half to himself. 'The grav-compensators aren't holding us. I'm going onto manual.'

His hand moved rapidly along a row of switches while the other took a firm grip on the central control column. 'Come on now . . . come on . . . ' he urged gently, almost crooning the words. 'Pull us back . . . come on . . . . '

Even to Maryatt, unable to read the displays, it was obvious they were accelerating. He held on tightly to the moulded armrests, his voice croaking with near panic. 'We're picking up space speed!'

'It's the gravity haul from Cephlon. I must have misjudged it and crossed into its ambit.' Ensor was gripping the column with both hands now, fighting the steadily increasing gravitational force.

'Can you get us out?' Maryatt said, his mouth dry.

'I'm on threequarter resist and she's not responding,' Ensor panted. pushing a lever forward with his thumb. 'Going to maximum!'

The narrow compartment reverberated with the whine and vibration of the craft's neutron power units as they sought to overcome the massive inertial drag of the giant red planet. The sound rose to a shrill protesting scream, the display panels flickering in a kaleidoscope of warning lights.

'You're going to rip her to pieces!' Maryatt shouted, his body rigid with fear.

The high-pitched noise had hit a sustained peak, and as Ensor battled to maintain control it slowly began to decrease as the ship assumed level flight.

'That's it . . . come on . . . steady now . . . .' Ensor murmured encouragingly. There was a faint note of relief in his voice. 'She's slowing. Compensators are beginning to hold.'

Maryatt watched tensely, his face white and strained.

'That's it . . . that's my girl . . . good . . . good . . . steady it up now.' Ensor allowed himself a fleeting grin towards his sweating companion. 'We're all right, she's coming back,' he reassured him. 'We're all right.'

Maryatt blew out his cheeks and slumped back. He held up his trembling hands and looked at them as if they didn't belong to him. 'Don't do that sort of thing too often, will you?' he begged. 'I'm a very nervous passenger.'

Ensor smiled ruefully. 'I'm a very nervous pilot — '

He got no further. The instrument panel erupted in a searing flash of flame, and the compartment was filled instantly with dense black choking smoke. Jagged pieces of twisted metal were flung outwards with the tremendous force of the explosion, injuring both men, and dimly, through all the confusion, could be heard the mounting shriek of tortured power units as the ship heeled over, totally out of control.

Semi-conscious from the blast, Ensor roused himself sluggishly, feeling the blood running freely from the deep gashes in his head and shoulders. He groped blindly towards the navigation log — a small heavily reinforced black box below the instrument panel — wrenched the connecting terminals from their sockets, and pushed the black box into the top of his coverall.

The smoke had cleared a little, and he was able to make out Maryatt's bleeding and unconscious body sprawled in his seat. Gathering all his strength, Ensor hauled himself across the narrow space, grabbed hold of the Medic's shoulders and dragged him towards the oval hatch leading to the rear storage compartment. He was halfway through with his cumbersome burden when the instrument panel spluttered and sparked with a fierce electrical discharge and there was another violent explosion — a billowing cloud of smoke streaked with tongues of flame enveloping them in furnace heat and scorching every hair on their bodies.

The crippled ship entered the atmosphere of Cephlon and began to burn up as it plunged towards the surface of the red planet.

Blake arrived on the Flight Deck to find the crew watching the scanner screen with mesmerized fascination. It took him less than a second to take it all in, striding forward to the central command position.

'What happened?'

'Not sure,' Jenna replied, sparing him a quick glance. 'Zen located her about five minutes ago. We put her on scanner trace to run a security check, then she suddenly went off course.'

'There was a flash a few moments ago,' Avon added. 'Could have been a neutron power unit going nova.'

Cally's large green eyes were fixed on the screen. 'Isn't there anything we can do to help them?' she asked gravely.

Blake shook his head. 'If they're still alive their only hope are the survival capsules.' He spoke to the master computer. 'Identification.'

'*The ship is a Spacemaster rocket Series 5. Four neutron power units with an optimum level nine thrust capacity. Its range capability is —* '

'Does she carry survival capsules?' Blake interjected.

'*Standard equipment specification lists two high-impact unpowered survival modules.*'

'She's entering Cephlon's atmosphere,' Vila chirped up, seeing a faint glow shimmer round the craft. 'Look, she's beginning to burn up!'

Jenna turned away, unable to watch the fiery destruction, and therefore didn't see the two tiny egg-shaped pods fall away from the doomed ship.

'The survival capsules!' Blake exclaimed. 'They've ejected!' He turned swiftly to Zen. 'Lock tracers onto those capsules. I want a firm fix on their impact location.'

'*Trace locked on,*' came the immediately reply.

'We're going down,' Blake decided at once. 'Jenna, Vila, Gan — get kitted up.' As they hurried away to the teleport section he faced the master computer. 'Surface conditions.'

'*The planet Cephlon has a breathable atmosphere with a high oxygen content. The radiation level is in excess of normal tolerance limits and prolonged exposure could result in tissue damage. Massive variations in temperature and humidity. Gravity is plus oh-five G.*'

'Life forms?'

'*There is no updated information. Early surveys refer to highly developed humanoid creatures with advanced technology. Logic circuits speculate that remaining life may have mutated through exposure to high radiation.*'

'None of that sounds good,' Avon remarked, looking at Blake meaningfully.

'We'll get down and back as fast as we can,' Blake promised him wryly, heading for the doorway. 'Have Zen give us the survival capsule landing coordinates.'

There was a bustle of activity in the teleport section as everyone prepared for the surface landing. Blake joined them, slipping quickly into his one-piece acrylic suit with its equipment pouches and strapping on the utility power belt and sidearm.

'Are we all set?'

150

'I think so,' said Jenna, and the other two nodded.

'We're going to make this fast,' Blake told Cally at the teleport control desk. 'The chances are that any survivors wouldn't have come through the landing impact.'

'But they might have,' Jenna countered. 'They could still be alive.'

'That's the only reason we're going down — but if we run into any kind of trouble we teleport back immediately. Is that understood?' Blake gestured them forward and the landing party moved into the transmission area, clipping on their bracelets.

Avon came in and handed a slip of paper to Cally, who began to set the variable markers on the hatched grid.

'The coordinates place both capsules within one square mile,' Avon informed them. 'That's about as accurate as we can get. We're teleporting you down right into the centre of the search area.'

'Got it,' Blake confirmed. 'Keep the circuits open and stay close to the teleport. Right, put us down . . . . '

The terrain was rugged: a series of rocky outcrops and small stunted trees on a bed of red sandstone that rose gradually to a steep cliff face about a quarter of a mile above them. They were on the lower slopes of a mountain scored with ravines and dried-out water courses. Beyond a ridge they saw a curling plume of black oily smoke, staining the pale sky like a dirty thumbprint.

'That must be the wreck of the ship,' Blake guessed. 'No point in checking that. We'll split into pairs and work a search pattern. Gan and Jenna, you cover that arca — ' He pointed lower down the slope to a jumble of dark rocks and sparse vegetation. 'Vila and I will work this side. And remember what I said . . . even a hint of danger and we teleport back.'

Jenna and Gan nodded their understanding and began picking their way down the shale-littered slope, descending into shallow gullies and over smooth slabs of sandstone that gave the appearance of having been exposed to an intense scorching blast.

Gan led the way, grunting with the exertion of keeping his balance on the treacherous surface. 'What exactly are we looking for?' he asked over his shoulder. 'I don't think I've ever seen an impact survival capsule.'

'They're sort of missile-shaped . . . no, more like an egg, I suppose.' Jenna was more nimble on her feet than the big man. 'They're built of energy-absorbing material. In theory you could drop one from the edge of inner space onto solid rock and the fall wouldn't even bruise the person inside.'

'Do they contain life-support systems?'

'Just a basic respirator, not much else.'

They reached the jumble of rocks, like huge dark brown pebbles thrown down in a heap by a giant hand, and found a way through to a small sandy depression beyond. Jenna dropped to one knee, pointing to where the soil had been gouged in a straight line, as if worked by a plough share.

'Gan, look at this.'

'Could be a landing track.'

Jenna followed the line with her eye. 'Runs that way.'

The gouged track extended some thirty yards, and there, at the base of an overhanging cliff face, lay the squat, cylindrical shape of the survival capsule, its surface blackened and charred by the fierce abrasion of re-entry.

'It's one of them!' Jenna cried, running towards it.

Gan trotted after her and came up as she was examining the strange egg-shaped object. 'How do you get it open?'

'The hatch should have been operated from the inside,' Jenna said worriedly. 'The fact that it hasn't doesn't look good. There should be an emergency release on the outer hull.' She moved round and located the release handle, inset into the curved surface. 'I've got it.' But when she attempted to operate it the hatch refused to budge.

Gan stepped forward, grasped the handle in his meaty fist and heaved with all his strength. The hatch resisted and then came open with a soft hiss as the air rushed in. The interior was padded and womblike, moulded in the shape of a man, and the man inside lay like a curled foetus, unmoving, his clothing damp with dried blood.

Jenna bent forward and removed the respirator mask from his face. She checked his pulse and searched for a heartbeat. Shaking her head, she straightened up and reported flatly, 'He's dead. I'd better tell Blake.'

She pressed the communicator button on her bracelet and Blake answered almost at once.

'We've found one of the capsules. The man inside is dead.'

'See if you can find any identification on the body. Then seal the capsule again.'

'Confirmed,' Jenna said, breaking contact.

Gan unzipped a side pocket and produced an I D folder which he handed to Jenna, then carried on searching.

'His name was Tal Maryatt,' Jenna said, flipping through it. 'Born on Epsilon Four. He was a senior space surgeon serving with Federation Security and based at Space Command HQ. There some visigraphs of a woman and two children . . . . '

She compressed her lips and quickly closed the folder, slipping it into her pocket.

'Nothing much else,' Gan muttered, standing up straight.

Jenna gazed at the dead man, lying in what was effectively his coffin, and said curtly, 'All right. Let's seal him up.'

Blake and Vila had found the other capsule, partly embedded in soft red sand on the edge of a small hollow. The hatch was open and Ensor had managed to raise himself before slumping forward, semi-conscious, against the outer hull. Together they lifted him out of the capsule and set him down gently on the ground.

'He's pretty far gone,' Vila said dubiously, looking at the scorched hair and eyebrows and the deep cuts on the man's head and upper body.

Blake pulled the small black box from the top of his coverall and placed it to one side. Checking the man's pockets, he came across a flat metal container about the size of a hip flask, inside which were two tiny metal discs sealed in a transparent gelatin-like substance.

'What are those? Vila asked curiously.

'Micro power cells, I think. But I've never seen any this small before.' Blake snapped the container shut and laid it beside the black box.

Ensor stirred and came to, grasping Blake's wrist feebly. 'Maryatt . . . Dr Maryatt,' he croaked, his eyes misted with pain.

'The man who was with you?'

Ensor nodded weakly, his breath fluttering through dry lips.

'We've found the other capsule,' Blake told him gruffly. 'I'm sorry . . . he's dead.'

Ensor took the news stoically, then in a flurry of panic felt for one of his pockets. 'The energy cells — '

'It's all right,' Blake calmed him. 'They're safe.'

'I've got to get them to my father on the planet Aristo,' Ensor gasped. 'Without them he's only got about four days . . . six at the most and then he'll die . . . . '

'Take it easy,' Vila said soothingly. 'Easy now.' He glanced up at Blake, exchanging a look of grim resignation.

'Get them to him,' Ensor murmured hoarsely. 'Promise me. Promise.'

'We'll do everything we can.'

'Navigation log.' Ensor gestured weakly towards the black box. 'It will give you all the flight directions you need — ' He winced as a spasm of pain coursed through his shattered body. Fighting against it, he struggled on, his voice thin with desperation. 'Tell him . . . the Federation have agreed to his terms . . . they'll pay a hundred million credits for Orac . . . . '

'Orac?' Blake leaned forward, his eyes narrowing with sudden interest. 'What is Orac?'

Whatever it was, the man was unable to tell him. He was dead.

5

Blake hadn't moved for at least five minutes, Jenna noted. He was seated before the communications console, his chin propped on his fist, staring pensively at the navigation log and slim metal container on the desk nearby. She leaned back in the flight chair, releasing the controls for just a moment while she wiped the perspiration from her forehead. The atmosphere seemed close and oppressive; it reminded her of the muggy feeling that precedes a thunderstorm.

Avon came onto the Flight Deck and Blake glanced up as if surfacing from some deep inner thought. Beckoning Avon to him, he swung round in the chair and spoke to the master computer.

'Zen. Supplementary to flight log data.'

'*Line one is linked and ready to accept.*'

'Avon, I want you to listen to this.'

'What is it?'

'Sit down and listen.' Blake picked up a hand microphone and pressed the RECORD button in its base. 'At time coordinate six-six-two *Liberator* was passing the planet Cephlon. Scanner systems located a space vehicle which was identified as a Spacemaster Series Five. There was an explosion on board and the ship went out of control. Cephlon's gravity pulled her down into the atmosphere and she started to burn up. Two life-support capsules ejected and our tracers followed them to impact. We teleported down and both capsules were found. In the first the crew member was dead. In the second a man called Ensor was badly injured. Before he died he gave me a box containing micro power cells. He insisted that we should take these to the planet Aristo, since without

155

them his father will die. He also spoke of something called Orac and claimed that the Federation were willing to pay one hundred million credits to obtain it. Verbal supplementary closes.'

'Well?' Avon said quizzically.

'If the Federation are willing to pay one hundred million, then Orac must be quite important,' Blake pointed out.

'Unless of course it's a magnificent swindle.' Avon's tone was derisive. 'But I suppose that's too much to hope for.' His pale hooded eyes widened fractionally. 'Are you all right?'

Blake was leaning forward, both hands pressed to his face. They were trembling slightly. 'I just felt a bit dizzy, that's all.' With an effort he shook it off and went on more alertly, 'My point is this — there's something we've missed. I can sense it.'

'I can't think what,' Avon shrugged. 'It all seems straightforward enough.' He nodded at the black box nearby. 'We know from the ship's log that it was returning to Aristo from Federation Headquarters. The other passenger was a doctor. They were carrying medical supplies. It all tallies with what Ensor said.'

Blake frowned, still not convinced. 'I'm not sure . . . . I think it's the importance the Federation are putting on Orac that bothers me.'

Jenna paused for a moment by his chair. 'I've switched to automatics. Something I want from my cabin,' she explained, moving towards the living quarters.

'Right, Jenna,' Blake said distantly. Both he and Avon were too preoccupied to notice that her face was flushed and she didn't seem altogether steady on her feet.

'Let's take another look at the scanner pictures of that ship on the main screen,' Blake suggested, standing up.

'They're not going to tell us anything we don't already know.'

'Perhaps not. But let's check it anyway.' Blake considered where to start, then nodded decisively. 'Zen. Run the scanner file from the moment we picked up visual contact with the Spacemaster ship.'

'*Confirmed. Retrieval systems operating.*'

'What exactly are you looking for?' Avon inquired, bemused by Blake's vague insistence that something was amiss.

'I'm not sure yet.'

While they were waiting for the pictures to come up, Vila wandered onto the Flight Deck and stood watching the large screen with them.

'There it is,' Avon said as the small two-seater craft appeared on the screen. 'Normal flight. No indication of any difficulty.'

'Just coming to the point where the motors go up,' Blake murmured, all his concentration focused on the ship, seemingly motionless, against the backdrop of the vast red planet.

There was a tiny flashpoint on the nose of the rocket that grew instantly into a consuming ball of fire, and Blake rapped out:

'Zen, hold it there! Right, now go back, slowly . . . .'

The screen showed the action in reverse until the precise moment when the flare of the explosion began.

'Stop,' Blake ordered. The picture froze. 'That's it!' He smacked his fist into his palm. 'Look, that's what was bothering me!'

'Huh?' Vila screwed up his face. 'I don't see anything special.'

Avon was quicker. 'It's in the wrong place,' he stated quietly.

'Exactly. The explosion's in the forward section. We thought it was a neutron burn-out, but that's nowhere near the engine housing.'

'All right,' Avon conceded, 'but it doesn't change anything, does it?'

Blake turned aside. 'Zen. I want the sensor readings for the moment of explosion. Full spectrum analysis.'

'What are you trying to prove?' Vila asked him querulously, baffled by all the fuss.

Blake faced them, his eyes shrewd and calculating. 'Ensor went to Federation Headquarters. He wanted medical assistance. But he also wanted to sell something of enormous value.'

'Orac,' said Vila.

'Right.'

'Whatever that is,' Avon muttered.

'We can presume the deal was made because he told us they were willing to pay a fantastic price for it. Now, they start on the return journey — '

'*The information you requested is now available.*'

'Let's have it.'

'*Sensor readings are as follows: the explosion registered one-point-three. Disturbance peaked at one-one-five. Spectral analysis of residual vapour confirms presence of Gemitan explosive.*'

'Conclusion?'

'*Probability is that a small explosive device was detonated in the gravity compensator control system.*'

'Sabotage!' Avon hissed under his breath.

Blake nodded, grim-faced.

Vila spread his hands. 'But why? he asked, perplexed.

Avon looked at Blake in mutual understanding. 'So the Federation can get hold of Orac without paying the hundred million.'

'That's about the only thing that would make sense,' Blake agreed soberly.

Vila was beginning to see the light. 'So they'll be on their way to pick up Orac as fast as they can go,' he surmised. 'And that's fairly fast . . . . '

'But not as fast as *Liberator,*' Blake said softly.

Avon's mouth twisted sardonically. 'Ever the optimist, Blake.'

They were interrupted by the appearance of Cally, who strode across the Flight Deck, her normally impassive face bearing signs of concern.

'Blake!'

'What is it?'

'Jenna. She's very sick. Gan is too. He has the same symptoms.'

158

'What's wrong with them?'

Cally held up a small electronic instrument with a gauge in the top surface and a short metal probe extending from the front. 'I want to run a test. Put your hand out.'

Blake did so and at once the device emitted a rapid ticking sound and the needle flicked across the dial. She ran the probe along Vila's hand and the result was the same.

'Just like the others. You've all absorbed heavy doses of radiation.'

'Radiation!' Vila stared wildly at the offending hand as if it didn't belong to him. Or wished desperately that it didn't. 'But how . . . ? All over?'

'The four of you went down to the surface of Cephlon,' Cally explained. 'You stayed too long, far beyond tolerance limits. You need treatment and you need it quickly — '

'Well, what are you waiting for?' Vila demanded heatedly. 'Let's get to the surgical unit.'

Avon held up his hand. 'Relax. You'll go onto a massive dose of de-contaminant drugs and within a day or — '

'Not possible.'

'Why not, Cally?' Blake asked.

'There are no decontaminant drugs on the ship. I have checked. There is nothing that will counter radiation sickness.'

'You're sure?'

'I'm sure.'

'Then our only hope is that they have a supply on Aristo,' said Blake, with rather more confidence than he actually felt.

'And if they don't?' Vila said gloomily.

'They will have.'

'But if they don't?' he persisted.

'They *will* have.'

Cally knew there was nothing to be gained by denying the reality of the situation. She said with quiet emphasis, 'There's no point in hiding it. Your condition will deteriorate rapidly. If you don't get drug treatment very soon, you will die.'

Gan was sleeping peacefully when Avon entered the rest room, his broad, heavily muscled body sprawled on a couch. There was a mist of perspiration on the big man's forehead and his breathing came in shallow audible gasps.

Avon crossed to the circular port and stared out at the inky blue-blackness of space, becoming lost in speculation so that he didn't hear the door open, and only looked round when Blake said quietly, so as not to disturb the sleeping Gan:

'I had Zen run through the reference banks. This Professor Ensor is a remarkable man. A very impressive list of achievements.'

Avon nodded, turning away from the window. 'I know. When he was eighteen years old he developed something called the Tarial Cell. It led to a whole new generation of computers.' He eased himself into a chair opposite Blake's. 'Every computer in the known worlds contains Tarial Cells. He developed and engineered a lot of radical new concepts in computer technology. Even the most advanced computers are based on his work. Come to think of it, I'm surprised the Federation ever let him go.'

'They didn't. Not exactly . . . .'

Both men glanced up as Cally came into the room.

'How are they?' Blake asked anxiously.

'Much the same.' Cally's expression was sombre. 'Until they get treatment the only change will be for the worse. How are you feeling?'

'At the moment, not too bad,' Blake replied, managing a faint grin. 'Who's at the controls?'

'Jenna.'

Blake looked towards the circular port where the rim of a planet could be seen, edging into view. 'Nearly there. Another hour.'

'Ironic,' Avon mused, shaking his head slowly. 'We're racing to deliver medical supplies to save a man's life in the hope he'll have medical supplies that will save yours.'

Blake disregarded such a morose line of thought. 'Zen

160

told me something else that would explain why he needs those energy cells,' he said. 'It appears that Professor Ensor took a vacation on a frontier planet. While there he suffered a massive heart attack. Medical facilities were primitive. The only available transplant was a mechanical heart powered by micro cells. They have a life of about forty Earth years . . . all of which happened about forty years ago,' he added meaningfully.

'Didn't they substitute an organic unit when he got back?' Cally asked.

'That's the point — he never did get back. He simply vanished. He and his four-year-old son just disappeared, and that was the last that was ever heard of them.'

'Until now,' Avon said.

'And all that time he was hiding away on Aristo,' Cally murmured.

Blake roused himself. 'Come on,' he grunted, nodding to the girl. 'We'd better get ready to teleport down.'

The obelisk rose sternly like a dark pointing finger on the edge of the steep sandy cliff overlooking the shore. Beneath a sullen sky that was massing with thunderclouds, the ocean swell moved sluggishly, bubbling and frothing in a pale yellow hue as the waves cascaded gently onto the shelving beach. At the base of the cliff, amidst what appeared to be the ruin of an ancient building, crouched a small, slim figure dressed in a tightly fitting field uniform complete with map-case, lightweight short-wave transmitter and sidearm. Surveying the immediate area with a calm methodical gaze, Servalan consulted the map in her gloved hand, raised her head and called out peremptorily, 'Travis! Here!'

He came through the ruined building, stepping over the blocks of masonry half buried in the sand, and dropped to one knee beside her.

'There it is,' Servalan said, pointing to a heavy iron ring inset into a large stone slab. 'The map was correct.'

Travis nodded without speaking, and brushing aside the sand and small pebbles that partially obscured it, he gripped the iron ring and heaved with all his strength. The slab was stuck fast with age and lack of use, and Servalan moved to help him, their combined effort only just sufficient to budge it. With a hollow grating sound like the rumble of distant thunder, the slab was slowly raised to an upright position.

A smell of dank putrefaction drifted up from the depths. Unclipping his torch, Travis shone it down into the hole, his mouth twisting in repugnance at what the beam revealed.

'There must be an easier way into the laboratory than this,' he scowled at her turning his head away from the evil stench of rotting seaweed and dead fish.

'The surface force barrier is impenetrable,' Servalan reminded him blandly. 'We must go under it.'

Travis nodded reluctantly. 'Let's see the old man's map again.'

Together they bent over the chart, Servalan tracing her finger from the point of entry. 'We go along this passage here . . . turn right at the junction and then straight on.'

'The passages begin to run below sea-level after that. Let's hope they're not flooded.'

'Let's get started.' Servalan folded the map and tucked it away.

Shining their torches ahead of them, they descended into the gloomy labyrinth via a shallow flight of stone steps leading down to a narrow tunnel that was ankle-deep in stagnant water. The walls were running with green slime and the foul odour was overpowering. Servalan shone her beam into the chill darkness.

'Travis . . . this way.'

They moved carefully along the tunnel, peering ahead, and hadn't gone very far when both experienced the odd feeling that they weren't alone. It was as if some other unknown presence was lurking near — and then, quite distinctly, they heard a soft hissing sound. It seemed to be all around them, a sibilant whisper emanating from the slimy walls.

Stumbling after Travis, Servalan's white pinched

nostrils detected another odour. It was the smell of her own fear.

Blake and Cally hurried onto the Flight Deck, fully kitted out for a surface landing. Picking up the flat metal container from the desk, Blake checked that the micro power cells were safe in their transparent envelopes, snapped the container shut and slipped it into his arm pouch. His faced showed concern as he looked towards Jenna at the controls: she had recovered slightly, though her cheeks still burned with fever.

'Are you going to be up to handling things here?'

Jenna gave him a brave smile. 'Assuming you don't take too long.'

Blake winked encouragingly and spoke briskly to the computer.

'Zen. Surface conditions on Aristo.'

The sequence of lights changed and steadied and the impersonal voice began, *'The land masses are arid, calcified and support only primitive plant life. Nine-tenths of the planet is covered by water which is highly acidic. The level of the oceans is constantly rising and now virtually covers all traces of the cities built by early civilizations.'*

'Life forms?'

'Life is evolving in the oceans and amphibian species have begun to develop.'

'Anything else?'

'This constitutes all available data.'

'At least there won't be too many natural hazards to deal with,' Jenna remarked hopefully. She gave her attention to the flight control panel, scanning the readings with a practised eye, then operated a series of controls. The deep throb of the engines dwindled to a low murmuring as the huge ship came within the ambit of the planet.

'Positional status?' Jenna asked the computer.

'Transit complete,' came the prompt reply. *'Liberator is in stationary orbit within teleport range of the planet Aristo. All circuits are . . . all circuits are . . .'* The voice began to

slur, dying away to a long-drawn-out grinding moan. ' . . . *all . . . circuits . . . are . . .*'

'Zen!' Jenna shouted in alarm. Swiftly she went through the emergency procedure, punching buttons with a mounting sense of desperation.

Blake bounded to her side, reaching out to repeat the emergency sequence on the control panel.

'It's no good, I've done all that,' Jenna said frantically.

The indicator lights on the curved fascia had faded away to nothing; and then, with startling suddenness, the central panel glowed vividly with a greenish light that pulsed hypnotically. From the speaker grille issued a voice none of them had heard before — a harsh nasal voice that sounded mechanical in origin.

'You will identify yourselves and state clearly the purpose of your intrusion.'

'Who are you?' Jenna demanded, watching the pulsing green glow.

'Specify recognition code,' Blake rapped out, but the voice totally ignored his request.

'I repeat: identify yourselves and state the purpose of your mission.'

Blake leaned across the flight control desk, hands braced apart. 'This is the spacecraft *Liberator*. We have medical supplies for somebody on this planet.'

'You will explain the circumstances governing your previous statement.'

'We went to the aid of a crashed space vehicle. Before the pilot died he asked us to deliver some micro power cells. He said they were vital to save his father's life.'

'Your explanation is satisfactory,' the voice said with machine-like infallibility. 'I am aware that you have teleport facilities. I will set coordinates for a surface landing. On arrival you will await further instructions. That is all.'

Blake straightened up, his eyes sparkling angrily. 'That's all, is it?' The smug assured tone infuriated him. 'Jenna, institute a thorough circuit check,' he ordered brusquely.

The vivid green glow blinked off with the same abruptness and Zen's indicator lights resumed their familiar pattern.

'*All circuits are now free and full function is restored.*'

'What happened?' Cally asked no one in particular.

Zen supplied the answer. '*Preliminary research indicates that all computer functions were temporarily under external control.*'

'That's impossible!' Jenna declared.

'*Logic units concur that it is impossible,*' Zen agreed urbanely.

'But it happened anyway,' Blake said sourly.

'*Logic units concur that it happened. Investigation of this paradox is continuing.*'

Jenna glanced up at Blake, her expression disturbed and fretful. 'I don't like it. A force that can take over our master computer could easily control the ship.'

'Well, we're not going to find out about it standing here,' Blake decided. He gave Cally a brief nod. 'You ready?'

'Yes, I am ready.'

'Jenna, set the automatics and then go to your cabin and rest.'

'What about you? Will you be all right?' Jenna said anxiously.

'I'm not going to stop long enough to think about it,' Blake answered, already moving towards the exit. 'Come on,' he urged Cally, and the girl followed him at the run.

Avon was standing at the teleport control desk when they entered the section, a look of blank amazement on his face. His hands were poised above the controls like a pianist who's forgotten how to play.

'Blake, look at this!'

'What is it?' Blake asked, striding forward.

'The locator grid,' Avon said faintly, staring at the panel. 'It's setting the coordinates . . . by itself.'

Blake stood beside him and watched the variable transparent markers moving smoothly to a new position, as if by remote-control.

'It looks as though our computer has been over-ridden again. It's being programmed from another source.'

'Maybe we should pull out while we still have a chance,' Cally suggested.

Blake looked dubious. 'Frankly, I doubt if we could even if we wanted to. From what we've seen already it's obvious that the force, whatever it is, could totally immobilize us.'

'Right, let's get on with it, shall we?' Avon proposed.

Blake and Cally moved into the transmission area, clipping on their bracelets.

'Try and stay near the teleport desk,' Blake called out. 'Just in case we have to get out fast.'

'I haven't any plans to go anywhere else,' Avon informed him with a fleeting smile. He touched the slide control tentatively, as if it might possess a life of its own, and slowly pushed it forward. When he raised his eyes, Blake and Cally had gone.

They were standing on the edge of a cliff facing an ocean that seemed curiously placid and lifeless. The waves breaking on the shore hissed and bubbled in a froth of pale yellow, and on the breeze was an acrid tang that reminded Blake of a chemical laboratory.

'What do you suppose that is?' Cally asked, touching his arm.

Blake turned, seeing the obelisk for the first time. A rectangular column of stone tapering to a blunt point.

'Some sort of marker,' he conjectured with a shrug.

Cally surveyed the empty horizon. 'Well, what do we do now?'

'Wait for further instructions. There isn't much else we can do. Let's take a look around.'

Cally wandered off a little way past the obelisk. She halted suddenly and called him across.

'What is it?' Blake asked, moving to her side.

'Watch.' Cally stretched out her hand nervously and then quickly retracted it as if she'd touched something.

Blake did the same and felt his hand come into contact

with a solid invisible wall. 'It's a force barrier.' His flat upright palm moved sideways through the air, trying to gauge the extent of it. 'Question is, are we on the outside unable to get in — '

' — or on the inside unable to get out?'

Blake nodded reflectively. His eye was suddenly caught by something. Way out across the ocean a tiny brilliant dot of light was racing towards them. Heading straight for the obelisk, it came at them from out of the dark sky and stopped directly above their heads, a small silver sphere remaining perfectly motionless in mid-air.

'You are carrying weapons. You will remove them.'

Again the same harsh nasal voice they had heard in the ship.

Blake glanced at Cally and then up at the gleaming satellite. 'We'd prefer to keep them with us . . . . '

'You will remove them.'

Blake shook his head. 'No,' he said mildly.

A thin beam of intensely pure light issued from the sphere and the ground at Blake's feet exploded, showering him with sand.

'We will remove them,' he agreed wryly.

They hardly had time to unfasten their belts and place their sidearms on the ground before the mechanical voice was urging them, 'You will make greater speed. Hurry! Hurry!'

Cally moved forward a couple of paces, her hand outstretched in front of her. 'How do we get through the force barrier?'

The sphere emitted a series of bleeps, squeaks and rapid ticking noises. Cally felt the barrier disappear and she was able to walk on, unimpeded.

'Versatile, isn't it?'

'Let's hope it's still around when we want to get out,' Blake remarked with a rueful sideways glance at her. He pressed the transmit button on his communicator and raised it to his lips.

'It is too late to contact your ship,' the satellite advised him curtly. 'Signal transmission through the energy screen is not possible. You will follow me.'

The sphere revolved on its axis and moved speedily away, Blake and Cally being obliged to break into a trot to keep up with it. After following the cliff-edge for some distance the sphere veered to the right, and upon reaching the spot they came across a narrow sandy path leading down to the beach. The yellow frothing breakers lisped against the shore, wafting a pungent smell of chemicals which caught at the back of the throat.

Ahead of them the sphere was hovering in a fixed position, and as they neared it the voice rang out, 'You will make haste and approach the transporter.'

'Transporter?' Blake frowned.

Near the base of the cliff, protruding straight out of the sand to a height of about ten feet, stood a gleaming black cylinder, its surface smooth and highly polished. Blake estimated it was about four feet in diameter and made of a thermoplastic-type material.

'Move forward,' the satellite commanded, hovering overhead. 'You will now enter the transporter.'

Blake and Cally examined the shiny black column, which was totally devoid of markings or indentations, honed to perfect smoothness.

'There's no door,' Blake pointed out rather irritably.

'You will enter the transporter,' the satellite repeated in the same harsh tone.

'Look, I'm getting fed up with taking orders from you,' Blake snapped, glaring balefully at the silver sphere. 'How are we supposed to get inside this thing?'

'The girl will go first. Move directly to the transporter.'

Shrugging slightly, as if to humour the satellite, Cally stood in front of the column and took a pace forward, and disappeared. It seemed to the astonished Blake that she had walked straight through the solid black shiny wall of the column and vanished inside.

Stepping up to it, he took one bold pace forward and found himself inside a translucent cylinder through which a faint green light filtered, similar to the experience of being underwater.

'I said that thing was versatile,' Cally remarked, rather bemused.

'Maybe we should try and capture it. Avon might like it as a pet.'

They both lurched a little as the floor of the cylinder seemed to drop away beneath them. There was hardly any sound — perhaps the faintest sigh of an air current — as the column began to descend, rapidly gathering speed, lights moving faster and faster beyond the translucent green wall as they plunged deep below the surface. It was impossible to say to what depth they travelled, though from the pressure both experienced on their eardrums it was quite considerable.

The subdued rush of the slipstream died away and they felt the cylinder gradually slowing down, jostling them slightly as it came to a halt.

'We seem to have arrived,' Blake observed, and the words had hardly left his mouth when the curved wall of the cylinder slid aside to reveal a dim passage stretching away before them. The air was cool and fresh, as if replenished regularly from above, and the passage itself was dry and clean, obviously in constant use.

Blake and Cally set off, pausing at a heavy iron door set solidly in the stonework. Finding it locked, they moved on until they came to a T-junction, wavering uncertainly while deciding which way to go.

'Shall we split up and search?' asked Cally, her face pale and angular in the murky light.

Blake considered for a moment and shook his head. 'We'd end up looking for each other as well as Ensor and Orac.' He peered ahead down the gloomy passage to their left. 'We'll try this one. Come on . . . .'

6

The beams of the torches picked out hanging curtains of green slime as Travis and Servalan ploughed grimly onwards through the network of dank, evil-smelling tunnels. In places the foul water, encrusted with chemical scum, was almost knee-high, and the stench bit at their throats and made their eyes sting.

Keeping as close behind Travis as she could, Servalan was struggling to retain her normal icily aloof composure. Ever since they had entered the tunnels a sense of dire foreboding had stolen upon her, feeling her flesh crawl at the sound of something hissing and slithering in the darkness just beyond the range of their torches.

Stumbling after him, Servalan felt her heart contract as the sound echoed all around, and she clutched Travis's arm in a sudden seizure of panic.

'Travis, listen! What is it?'

Travis turned and she saw that his forehead was clammy and shining wet in the reflected light of the torch. 'I don't know, but it's been behind us since we started.'

Servalan suppressed a shudder. 'Let's keep going,' she said huskily, her apprehension making the words stick in her throat.

They carried on in grim, determined silence until up ahead Travis's torch illuminated what appeared to be a solid wall of slippery black boulders.

'The tunnel's blocked. Looks like a rockfall.'

'Can we get through?' Servalan asked anxiously.

'I'll go and check.'

Servalan waited nervously as Travis splashed ahead and began examining the rockfall. It might have been her imagination, she couldn't tell, but now the hissing and slithering noises were nearer than ever, and she kept glancing back fearfully over her shoulder, her body tense as if expecting some . . . thing to leap at her out of the gloom at any moment.

It was with heartfelt relief that she saw Travis wading back through the stagnant water.

'The roof looks as though it might cave in any second.'

'We knew there would be risks,' Servalan reminded him shortly.

'Let's just hope they're justified.'

'They are. When we deliver Orac to the Federation they will be very grateful and very generous. And what's more, the rewards and credits will be *ours*. Ours alone.'

Travis nodded, setting his jaw determinedly, and turned back towards the rockfall. 'Keep watch. I'm going to try and get through.'

Servalan watched as he began to clamber gingerly over the slippery rocks, the beam of his torch waving erratically with the awkwardness of his movements. She saw his shoulders outlined against a small gap, and a moment later the light dimmed and vanished completely as he squirmed his way through. Alone in the tunnel, with the only sound that of dripping water, Servalan could feel the cold, clinging dampness of fear bathing her face and neck. She breathed slowly, the air shuddering in her chest, somehow more afraid now that the hissing sound had stopped and there was only the echoing *plink-plonk-plink* of water to fill the eerie silence.

She looked fearfully towards the rockfall and called out tentatively, 'Travis?'

Silence and blackness shrouded everything.

'Travis!' Servalan called, her voice thin and high with a panic that was threatening to engulf her. And again: 'Travis!!'

Something had slithered behind her. Servalan spun round, hardly daring to raise her torch, and as she did so, staring wildly, something reptilian with shiny green scales lunged forward out of the darkness and clutched at her leg with clawlike feelers. She caught a glimpse of its face, bulbous eyes and horny plates of bone enclosing a slit of a mouth, and felt the creature dragging at her, trying to pull her over.

Fighting it off with a strength born of desperation, Servalan screamed at the top of her voice, lashing out in blind panic.

'Travis! Travis! Help me!'

The creature was too strong, it was dragging her down into the foul water. She felt her strength ebbing away, the prehensile claws digging into her flesh, and just as her knees were about to give way there came the booming blast of a high-energy weapon, deafening in the confined space.

The impact flung the creature backwards, almost ripping it in two, and the next moment Travis was wading towards her, a wisp of exhaust gas curling from his handgun. He gripped her arm tightly, preventing her from falling.

'Are you hurt?'

Servalan couldn't speak. She shook her head weakly, leaning on his arm and trying to gather together her shattered nerves. Travis waited until she was able to stand unsupported and went to take a closer look. He shone his torch down onto the scaly body and turned it over with his boot. The bulbous eyes gazed vacantly at the ceiling, the slitted mouth hung open.

'What is it?' Servalan asked numbly, her mouth pulled down in a grimace of loathing.

'I don't know. Some kind of amphibious lizard.' Travis moved past her along the tunnel, pointing his torch ahead. 'We can get through, just. You have to crawl, but it widens out further on.'

Servalan trailed after him, still shaken, and Travis, sensing her fear and reluctance, glanced round with a superior grin. The knowledge of his own strength and her discomfiture were pleasurable to him.

'The . . . "rewards and credits" . . . remember?' he reminded her snidely. And then, still grinning, 'I'll go first, shall I?'

Stung by his words and his manner, Servalan regained some of her icy composure. Asserting her authority, she gazed up at him with narrowed eyes and snapped, 'No, Travis. You will follow me.'

Travis stood aside, allowing the Supreme Commander to precede him, and with a last look behind clambered after her over the slippery black rocks.

The passage ended abruptly in a smooth, shiny black wall made of a similar material to the translucent cylinder. There was no visible sign of a means of access.

'Looks the same as the transporter,' Cally observed.

Blake moved forward to examine it, and without any warning the entire gleaming wall slid silently open.

'And just as disconcerting,' Blake retorted, stepping through into what at first sight appeared to be a bizarre amalgam of laboratory, living quarters and tropical hothouse. A closer study confirmed the impression. Workbenches cluttered with all manner of scientific instruments and equipment were set amongst a jungle of dense green shrubbery, huge exotic flowers swaying on slender stalks and vines trailing in haphazard profusion. Here and there were items of cane furniture — chairs and low recliners — and in an alcove behind a bead curtain they could see an unmade bed scattered with books and clothing. The tremulous twitter of birdsong filled the air, coming from a cage made of cane suspended from the ceiling on a chain.

'Blake!'

Cally was pointing at a metal rack. Lying amongst an assortment of electronic components was the small silver sphere that had led them to the transporter.

Blake shook his head in mute wonder as he looked around, rather taken aback at finding this scientific grotto deep beneath the ocean.

'At last!'

Pushing his way through the foliage, a white-haired man in his sixties shambled forward with both hands outstretched. He was sloppily dressed in a crumpled white shirt and baggy trousers tied up with string, and wore a pair of grimy white sneakers, without laces, on his bare feet.

'The energy cells! Have you brought the energy cells?'

Blake blinked at him in surprise. 'Yes . . . yes . . . we've got them. Are you all right?'

'Of course I'm not all right!' Professor Ensor snapped irascibly. 'If I was all right I wouldn't need you. And it certainly took you long enough to get here. Typical of you morons in physical medicine.'

'You don't understand — ' Cally started to say, but Ensor carried on, unabated.

'It always has to be a mercy dash, doesn't it? It's not enough to simply arrive, do your work and get out. It always has to be a drama.'

'We got here as quickly as we could,' Blake told him evenly.

Ensor waved him aside irritably and reached up to the birdcage, twiddling a dial in its base. The strident birdsong faded to a soft background cheeping, and Blake saw that the cage contained a mechanical replica of a nightingale. He looked at Cally, his expression of wry amazement mirroring hers.

'I don't want to hear your feeble excuses,' Ensor went on, shuffling across the laboratory and unbuttoning his shirt. 'Let's get on with it. I've developed a system of electronic anaesthesia that I shall administer myself. I won't need your filthy drugs. You can start carving me up as soon as you like.'

Cally took a step forward. 'You must listen to us — '

'You'll have to work quickly — an implant operation can't be done in ten minutes, you know,' Ensor said, paying no heed. He had opened his shirt to reveal a long scar down the left-hand side of his chest. Enclosed by a pattern of cross-hatched stitching in the region of his heart, a small multi-pointed socket protruded about half an inch. Standing before the workbench, he switched on an instrument similar to a radio transmitter, a row of circular gauges recessed in the grey metal fascia, and picked up a coiled lead connected to the back of the instrument.

'Professor, what are you doing?' Blake inquired, patient and yet puzzled at the same time.

'The last check I made showed there was very little in reserve,' Ensor rambled on, half to himself. 'The instrument is not entirely accurate, but it will give us some indication.' He plugged the lead into his chest and leaned forward short-sightedly to read the gauges. 'There! You see! I suppose you enjoy this sort of thing . . . boosts your egos to have the power of life and death. Adds to the mystique with which you medics like to surround yourselves.'

Unplugging the lead, he turned to face them. 'Now, which of you is the surgeon?' And when Blake and Cally only stared at him, nonplussed, went on bad-temperedly, 'Come on, come on, speak up. Which one of you is the butcher?'

Blake spread his hands. 'We're not medics, I'm afraid, Professor . . . .'

'What!' Ensor's bushy white eyebrows shot up in blank consternation.

Cally explained quickly. 'We went to the aid of a crashed spacecraft. One of the crew was dead, the other was dying, but before he died he asked us to get these to you urgently.'

Blake held up the metal container and opened it to show the micro power cells in their transparent sheath.

The news affected Ensor profoundly. His shoulders sagged and he stared emptily at the floor, suddenly seeming older than his sixty-four years.

'Both men dead you say?' he murmured, raising his head slowly to look at them.

Blake nodded stiffly.

'One of them was my son,' Ensor said, a catch in his voice. He turned away, touching the side of his face in a vague absent-minded manner.

'We are very sorry,' Cally said gently. 'He tried desperately to reach you. He did everything he possibly could.'

'Such a waste . . . death is such a waste. He had a good mind.' Ensor shook his head as if at some sober speculation. 'It's always too late, isn't it? I wonder if he knew how much I loved him . . . . '

'I think he did,' Blake assured the old man quietly.

Ensor sighed and glanced up. 'I'm sorry if I snapped at you. It's just my way. Thank you for doing what you could to help.'

'We were hoping that you might be able to help us,' Cally said anxiously.

'What is it you want?'

'Three of my crew and myself who went down to help your son were exposed to radiation,' Blake told him. 'Without decontaminant drugs the sickness will get progressively worse until . . . . '

'Oh, nothing easier,' Ensor said at once, gesturing to the back of the laboratory. 'A whole cabinet of drugs over there. Take what you want.' He wrinkled his nose disparagingly. 'Can't stand drugs myself. Filthy things.'

Cally went swiftly to where he had indicated, pushing through the broad shiny fronds of a giant rubber plant.

Blake snapped his fingers excitedly as a new plan occured to him. He faced the Professor and said urgently, 'Listen, how much time do you have before those energy cells fail completely?'

'Well, I'm not sure. As I told you, the instrument is not entirely accurate.' Ensor jutted out his lower lip. 'Thirty minutes . . . at the absolute outside, a couple of hours . . . . '

'Then there's still a chance,' Blake stated firmly. 'If we could get you up to our ship we might be able to carry out the implant ourselves. Our computer could instruct us.'

'You have the facilities to perform such an operation?' Ensor asked alertly, a faint glimmer of hope in his eyes.

'*Liberator* has one of the best-equipped surgical units you've ever seen.'

'It might just be possible, I suppose.'

'We can try. Come with us and you've got a chance. Stay here and you'll certainly die.'

It took only a moment for Ensor to reach a decision. He

nodded briskly. 'I'll do it. It's going to be hard, though, leaving this place — ' he swept his hand round the cluttered greenhouse of a laboratory ' — I've been here forty years.'

'Put this on,' said Blake, taking a bracelet from his hip pouch.

'What is it?'

'If you'll turn off the surface force barrier we can teleport you directly from here.'

'Not practical,' Ensor said promptly.

'Why not?'

'If I disconnect the force barrier now it'll be five hours before it dissipates. I haven't got five hours. We must go up to the surface.'

Cally returned, grinning broadly, and held up a pack of black capsules. 'Blake, I've found them. There's enough for everybody.' She had removed one of the capsules and offered it to him with a beaker of water. 'Here, take this.'

Blake slipped the capsule into his mouth and washed it down. Cally had already noticed that his eyes were feverish and that bubbles of perspiration had formed on his upper lip. The lines of strain as he stubbornly resisted the illness were evident at the corners of his mouth.

'I'm ready,' Ensor said, wrapping a creased white jacket round his narrow shoulders. 'Let's get moving.'

Blake held up his hand. 'Wait a minute — there is something else. What about Orac?'

'Orac!' Ensor exclaimed, as if referring to an old friend. 'We can't leave Orac here!' He bustled away and began shifting a pile of cluttered equipment on the floor next to the workbench.

'That was the message we were to give you,' Cally said, trying to peer over his shoulder. 'Your son said the Federation were willing to pay a hundred million for Orac.'

'They're willing to pay that, are they?' Ensor chuckled gruffly. 'Why, he's worth ten times that much! Now, come on, young woman, help me with this . . . . '

He was bent over, struggling to lift something. Cally

stooped beside him, prepared to lend a hand, and then slowly straightened up, her wide green eyes showing disbelief, even dismay.

'That is Orac?' she said haltingly.

Blake came to look and saw a crude metal frame, open on all sides, filled with a hotch-potch of clumsily wired solid-state circuitry, a maze of cables and various odd components apparently stuck in at random. It looked for all the world like the first attempt of an amateur technician to construct something from bits and pieces he just happened to find on his shelves. Altogether a very unpromising botched-up job that didn't seem capable of even the most basic electronic task.

'A hundred million for that?' Blake said, unable to keep the incredulity out of his voice.

'It is a computer . . . ?' Cally ventured timidly.

'It most certainly is not!' Ensor objected in a tone of outrage. 'It is a brain! A genius! It has a mind that can draw information from every computer containing one of my Tarial Cells! Orac has access to the sum total of all the knowledge of all the known worlds.'

Blake struggled to equate this statement with the amateurish box of tricks before him. 'You mean it can draw information from other computers without any direct link?' he asked sceptically.

'Precisely that,' Ensor said proudly. 'Now, do you want to stand here and listen to a lecture or might you consider it more important to try and sustain my life? Come on, help me to put Orac in its box.'

Exchanging bemused glances, Blake and Cally fitted the contraption into a lightweight aluminium container with a hinged lid and a handle at either end. Before snapping the lock, Ensor removed a small serrated disc from the guts of the machine and handed it to Blake.

'Perhaps you'd better take charge of this.'

'What is it?'

'It's a simple control device that activates Orac. Use it sensibly and Orac will advise you on every detail of the operation you intend to perform. Now . . . shall we go?'

Carrying the container between them, Blake and Cally made for the door, and were about to leave the laboratory when Ensor held up his finger and turned back.

'Just a minute . . . . I'll be right with you.'

He shuffled across to a large overhanging frond and traced his fingers along its delicately ribbed surface. 'Good-bye, my plants, I'm going to miss you,' he whispered tenderly, and gazing with affectionate eyes at the verdant greenery all around, murmured, 'The only real vegetation on this whole benighted planet . . . . '

'Professor — ' Blake called, waiting impatiently by the door.

Ensor awoke from his moment of fond reflection and started to leave, but turned back immediately and went over to the birdcage.

'I almost forget you, my little pet . . . . '

'Professor Ensor!'

'Good-bye, good-bye . . . . ' Ensor waved, bidding them a last farewell. 'I'll be back soon. Very soon.'

Travis stepped back from the iron door, his face running with sweat. Taking a black kerchief from his breast pocket he wiped his forehead and neck, shaking his head wearily.

'It's no good,' he told Servalan bleakly, 'it won't shift. Locked solid.'

'What are you going to do?

'I'm going to use a charge. It might warn him we're here, but there's no alternative.' He unzipped a side pocket and took out a small magnetic charge which he attached to the door near one of the massive hinges. Setting the pointer to prime it, he backed down into the tunnel, shepherding Servalan out of harm's way. 'Further back . . . take cover . . . it's a neutron-powered charge.'

They crouched down some considerable distance away, hugging the wall, but even so the shock-wave of the explosion hit them with stunning force. For several moments the tunnel reverberated with a rolling boom of thunder, and as it died away Travis wiped the dust from his face and started to move forward, urging Servalan to follow.

The iron door had been blown through into the passage beyond where it lay buckled and still smoking. Travis stepped through the shattered gap, and drawing his sidearm began to advance cautiously along the passage in the direction of the laboratory.

The sound of the explosion brought Blake and the others to a dead halt. It was near enough for them to feel a blast of hot air, as if someone had suddenly opened a furnace door in their faces.

'What was that?' Ensor demanded in a shocked whisper.

'Back to the lab!' Blake ordered. 'I'll take a look.'

He relinquished his hold on the container to Ensor, who with Cally's help struggled back with it the way they had come. Cally noted with concern that Ensor's face was grey and his breathing was wheezy and shallow.

Blake scouted ahead, and turning a corner saw Travis not twenty yards away with Servalan close behind. Firing from the hip, Travis loosed off an energy bolt that exploded against the wall above Blake's head, showering him with pulverized rock. Then Blake was off and running, hearing the thud of Travis's boots pounding after him.

Reaching the laboratory a second or two behind Cally and Ensor, Blake slammed the control switch with his fist, shutting the black door practically in Travis's snarling face.

'Weapons?' Blake snapped.

'I disapprove of weapons,' Ensor replied, his face ashen.

'So do I,' Blake told him grimly, 'but I disapprove of being killed even more.'

Cally's eyes darted round the laboratory. 'Is there another way out of here?'

'No . . . . ' Ensor hesitated, then nodded vaguely. 'Well, there is another way. We could get into the tunnels of the old city — '

'Come on, then,' Blake said impatiently.

'But it's not safe — '

'It will be safer than here. Show us.'

Ensor led them through the shrubbery to a round iron manhole built solidly into the rear wall. Judging from its rusted appearance it hadn't been used in decades.

'I think it's locked,' Ensor said absently.

'Get it open.'

Ensor ruffled his shock of white hair and looked pensive. 'The key . . . ' he mused, patting the pockets of his jacket, 'now where did I put the key?'

Travis stood powerless before the black door, glaring in rage and frustration at its gleaming, unblemished surface.

'Stand clear!' he rasped, pushing Servalan back with his hand, and aimed point-blank at the centre of the door. The searing blast blew the door inwards and Travis charged into the laboratory through a swirling haze of blue smoke.

Whirling round, ready to fire, it took him only a moment to realize that it was empty. At once he began searching for the other exit, but Servalan's icy command cracked out like a whiplash.

'Travis, forget Blake! Look for Orac!'

'I don't see it,' Travis fumed, stalking through the hanging greenery. 'Blake must have taken it. Give me the map.'

Servalan unfolded the map on the workbench and they bent over it, Servalan's gloved finger stabbing down on their position.

'The laboratory . . . we're here. Now in order to reach a surface exit they have to follow this tunnel.' Her finger traced the route. 'It's a long way. So if we go back the way we came, we could be on the surface first — waiting for them.'

Travis snatched up the map and stuffed it into his pocket. 'Come on, let's go,' he barked, already halfway to the door. Servalan strode after him, the scent of the kill in her nostrils.

7

Jenna was dozing over the teleport control desk when Avon hurried in, dressed and fully kitted-out for a surface landing, and shook her awake. It took her a moment to get her bearings, blinking groggily into Avon's alert face and then past his shoulder to where the sleeping Gan was sprawled awkwardly in one of the reclining chairs.

'What is it?' she mumbled. 'What's the matter?'

'Cally and Blake. They've been down too long — they must have run into trouble.' Avon looked at her grimly. 'See if you can wake Gan.'

He turned away to leave the section as Jenna struggled to her feet and moved listlessly to shake Gan's shoulder.

'Gan! Come on, wake up.'

He grunted and opened his eyes blearily. 'What? What's wrong, Jenna?'

'Something's happened to Blake and Cally.'

She looked up as Vila came in, zipping himself into a one-piece coverall, his movements slow and befuddled as if just having been roused from a deep sleep.

'Where is he?' Vila inquired hazily.

'We don't know,' Jenna answered.

'He woke me up,' Vila said in an aggrieved tone.

'Blake woke you up?' said Gan dully, only gradually coming to his senses.

'Avon did!' Vila snapped irritably. He wobbled back a pace as Avon bustled in and tossed a power belt and handgun to him. 'What are you up to?' he asked, frowning vaguely.

'You and I are going down to the surface. Put the belt on.'

Vila's eyes sharpened into focus. 'Are you out of your

mind? I'm finding it hard enough to stay on my feet — '

'Then crawl,' Avon said shortly, totally without sympathy. And then in a low, dangerous voice, 'Put-the-belt-on.'

Vila held up his hand placatingly and did as he was told.

'Gan, you stay here with Jenna,' Avon instructed, strapping on his own sidearm. 'Make sure one of you stays awake long enough to get us back up.'

'Right,' Gan affirmed.

'Avon, listen to me,' Jenna implored him. 'There's nothing you can achieve by going down there — '

'I'm not just going to sit here when they could be in trouble,' Avon shot back, his lean face filled with resolve. 'Get ready to put us down.' He chivvied Vila forward into the transmission area, taking some tiny white tablets from his pocket and pressing them into Vila's hand.

'What are these?'

'Energy pills. They should help — for a while, anyway.'

Jenna went to the control desk. 'Ready?'

'Get on with it,' Avon said stonily.

Ensor was leading the way, and to Blake and Cally it seemed that their progress through the tunnels was agonizingly slow. Even with the cumbersome weight of Orac between them, they felt they could have speeded up the pace if only the professor hadn't been in such poor physical shape.

Several times he had to pause and rest, leaning weakly against the wall, holding his hand to his chest and gasping to regain his breath.

'How much further?' Cally asked him as yet again they were obliged to halt while he tried to recoup his failing strength.

'Some way yet . . . . ' Ensor closed his eyes and moistened his dry lips. 'Look, I can't go on . . . I shall have to rest soon . . . . '

'We should keep moving,' Cally said worriedly. 'They could be close behind us.'

'Without weapons we won't stand a chance,' Blake agreed. He peered ahead along the gloomy tunnel. 'I've got an idea. You two keep moving. I'm going to stay here and try to bring the roof down — block them off.'

Cally seemed doubtful. 'Perhaps it would be better if we stayed together,' she suggested.

'Let's do it my way, Cally.'

The girl nodded and with Professor Ensor began lugging the heavy metal container through the tunnel, leaving Blake to wrestle with a jutting piece of masonry that was supporting the roof.

Cally tried to take as much of the weight as she could, keenly aware that Ensor was labouring painfully, using up his last shreds of strength. They struggled on for a while, their torchbeams slicing through the chill darkness and reflecting in dull gleams against the dank, sweating walls.

'Wait . . . ' Ensor gasped hoarsely, setting down his end of the container. 'Wait a minute, I have to rest . . . . '

He sank down onto his haunches and leaned back wearily, his face chalk-white with the strain of his exertions. Cally watched him, gnawing her lip, and then glanced back the way they had come in the hope of seeing Blake heading towards them. The tunnel was an empty black hole. She was becoming apprehensive at the pervading silence and darkness, wondering if perhaps he needed assistance.

Suddenly she stiffened, all her senses alert. A faint sound, not far away . . . as of something whispering or hissing softly.

'What was that?'

Ensor opened his eyes and said drably, 'There are creatures that live down here. Phibians.'

'Are they dangerous?'

Ensor lifted his shoulders and let them slump back. 'I don't think they'll harm us.'

Cally stared into the darkness, worried about what had become of Blake. She came to a snap decision and bent towards Ensor.

'Will you be all right?'

'Yes,' he mouthed, closing his eyes again.

'I'll be back,' Cally said, starting off down the tunnel.

It might have been her imagination, but it seemed that the hissing sound was getting louder. Curiously, it didn't appear to be coming from any one direction; it was all around — a sly, sibilant echo that turned the complex of tunnels into a vast whispering gallery.

Keeping the beam of her torch on the ground to watch out for hidden obstacles, Cally failed to see the creature poised on the ledge above her, the air hissing softly through the gill-like apertures in its neck. She knew nothing of its lurking presence until the sudden impact of its hard, scaly body sent her reeling forward and a pair of horny pointed claws clamped themselves round her throat.

With the creature's full weight on top of her, Cally managed a single piercing scream before its grip locked tight, throttling her cry of terror. The Phibian bore down, its huge bulbous eyes like glass spheres in the light of the torch that had been knocked from Cally's fingers. The apertures in its neck opened and closed rapidly as it exerted more pressure, the hissing of its foul breath loud in her ears.

Another light flickered in the darkness beyond, and through the pounding of blood in her head Cally dimly heard running footsteps as Blake raced along the tunnel and hurled himself at the creature. Dragging it from her, he swung the scaly head directly into the stone wall, and as the Phibian collapsed he followed up the attack with a rock, killing it with a single accurate blow to the base of the skull.

'Come on, Cally!' Blake gasped, hauling the girl to her feet, and together they staggered back to where Ensor and Orac awaited them.

'Check the way ahead is clear,' Blake rapped out, pushing her forward.

Cally hadn't gone a dozen yards when she saw a pale shaft of light and a flight of stone steps leading up to the surface.

'Blake, look!'

Blake nodded triumphantly and knelt before Ensor, shaking him by the shoulder to rouse him from his exhaustion.

'Professor Ensor! Ensor! We've made it!'

But Ensor didn't respond, and when Blake turned the white haggard face towards him he saw that time had finally run out. Ensor was dead.

Cally stood beside Blake as he straightened up and they both gazed down at the crumpled figure slumped in an awkward heap against the wall.

'I am sorry,' Cally murmured sadly. 'Just a little longer and we might have saved you . . . .'

Blake slammed the iron trap door shut and rolled a large boulder on top of it. He wiped his hands on his coverall and trudged across the sand to where Cally was standing wearily by the metal container, her angular face showing signs of exhaustion. They were both near the limit of their endurance, he realized.

Blake found a faint grin from somewhere. 'Call *Liberator*. Let's get out of here.'

Cally pressed the communicator button and raised the bracelet to her mouth, but before she could speak the ground at her feet erupted in the blast of an explosion. Blake spun round to see Travis and Servalan running down the cliff path towards them, the lethal destructor beam built in to Travis's arm still levelled menacingly at them.

'Good-bye, Blake,' Travis snarled as he came up, baring his teeth in a smile of mocking triumph. He stood arrogantly, legs braced apart, watching with undisguised pleasure as Blake and Cally raised their hands above their heads, defenceless and at his mercy.

'Travis — wait!' Servalan ordered curtly, striding forward.

'I have waited too long,' Travis growled, his single dark eye not leaving Blake for a second.

'He's the bonus, Travis. Orac is the prize.' Servalan addressed Blake coolly. 'Where is Ensor?'

'Ensor, like his son, is dead.'

Servalan nodded indifferently. 'It was to be expected. He survived longer than we thought possible.' She gestured haughtily towards the metal container. 'Orac — that is what we came for. If it does only half of what was promised it will give the Federation greater power than it's ever known.'

'What are you going to do with us?' Cally asked defiantly.

'What do *you* think I'm going to do?' Travis taunted her.

'I think you're going to kill me, Travis,' Blake said quietly. 'With or without orders from the Supreme Commander.'

'. . . with orders, Blake,' Servalan corrected him silkily. She gave a curt nod. 'All right, Travis. Go ahead.'

Aiming his gloved fist with its lensed rings directly at Blake's chest, Travis gave a smile of gloating satisfaction as he prepared to fire. There was a flash of intense white light from the arm followed by the crack of an explosive report and Travis's hand disintegrated in a smoking tangle of fused components and wires dangling from the scorched leather sleeve of his uniform.

'Don't move!' Avon rose from a kneeling position and advanced towards them, his handgun still smoking.

'Good shot, Avon,' Blake congratulated him.

'I was aiming for his head,' Avon said impassively.

Vila scrambled down the cliff. 'You certainly took your time,' he chided them crossly. 'What have you been up to?'

Cally glanced at Blake. 'We had a few minor problems.'

'Did you bring the decontaminants?'

'Yes.' Cally patted her pockets. 'We got them.'

'Tell them to bring us up,' Blake said to Vila.

'Jenna, stand by,' Vila said into his communicator.

Travis was glaring at Blake, his face contorted with raging fury. 'Well — what are you waiting for?' he demanded frenziedly. 'Why don't you kill us?'

Avon raised his handgun and Blake waved it away. 'No, I've got a better idea,' he proposed, a glint of crafty amusement appearing in his eyes. 'We'll get a message through to the Federation and tell them that you let us take Orac . . . . '

Travis and Servalan stiffened.

'I'm quite sure they'll be fascinated by your explanation.'

Alone on the beach, Servalan turned balefully towards Travis. She was white to the lips and trembling with suppressed anger, and would have spat in his face had she possessed full control of her faculties. She tried to speak, but found no words and, spinning on her heel, she stormed away across the sand.

Travis followed in her wake, a broken man in more than just the sense that sheared wires and blobs of metal trailed from his shattered arm.

'You want to give it a try?'

'Why not?' Blake shrugged, handing the small control disc Ensor had given him to Avon. 'Activator,' he explained.

Avon bent over the maze of components in its open metal frame and inserted the control device into a central slot. Everyone looked eagerly towards the machine, but Orac did nothing more spectacular than emit a faint, rather insipid glow.

'For a hundred million credits you'd expect it to do something more than light up,' Jenna said tartly.

'Try kicking it,' Vila suggested.

'Are you sure it's switched on?' asked Gan.

'Of course I'm "switched on",' said a voice in a pettish, irritable tone. 'Having depressed the activator button, what else would you expect?'

Cally looked at Blake. 'It is his voice,' she said wonderingly.

'Exactly as though Ensor were speaking,' Blake agreed, nodding.

'Surely it's obvious even to the meanest intelligence that during my development I would naturally become endowed with aspects of my creator's personality — '

'The more endearing aspects by the sound of it,' Avon commented dryly.

'Possibly,' Orac conceded loftily. 'However, similarities between myself and Ensor are entirely superficial. My mental capacity is infinitely greater.'

'Modest, isn't he?' Jenna said.

'Modesty would be dishonesty,' Orac rejoined at once.

'What's wrong with being dishonest?' Vila wanted to know, slightly affronted.

'Is that a question?'

'Yes!'

'The question is futile,' Orac said dismissively. 'Were I to say that I'm incapable of dishonesty, how would you know if I was being dishonest or not?'

'A question for a question!' Blake observed, enjoying the little philosophical game. 'You're capable of evasion, anyway.'

Vila, for one, had already formed his opinion. 'I think I've heard enough. I don't like him,' he stated flatly. 'Orac, be a good junk heap — shut up.'

'I agree with Vila,' Cally declared.

'Define the words "shut up",' Orac said imperturbably.

Blake helped him out. 'Stop talking. Do not speak. Be silent.'

'That is better,' Orac said patronisingly. 'Our relationship will be best served if your statements are free of ambiguity.'

Gan made a sour face and rose to his feet. 'Switch him off and let's get back to work,' he said, bored.

'No, wait a minute,' Blake insisted as everybody started to get up. 'We might as well find out what he *is* capable of.' He leaned towards the machine. 'Orac, what are your limits?'

'They have not yet been defined. My knowledge is virtually infinite. My secondary ability is to process that knowledge logically and make accurate predictions.'

'Are you saying you can see into the future?' Cally said in plain disbelief.

'The words "future", "present", "past", and "time" are meaningless,' Orac stated unequivocally.

'Define "meaningless",' Avon prompted.

'I have the capacity to predict events that have not yet taken place.'

'That's not what I asked.'

'In the circumstances the question is meaningless,' Orac said blandly, obeying only those rules of logic that he felt were important.

'That's ridiculous,' Blake said bluntly. 'Give us a demonstration.'

' "Demonstrate" as a command is insufficient.'

'What does he mean?' Gan frowned.

'He means that, like Zen, he needs specific instructions,' Avon explained.

'Instructions are not needed if commands are succinct,' Orac corrected him pedantically.

'I'm getting tired of this,' Vila sighed. 'Go on, predict something,' he challenged jeeringly.

The machine was silent for a moment, as if cogitating. 'I will project an image on your scanner screen.'

'Go on, then, show us,' Jenna said sceptically.

Orac ticked and whirred to himself and as everyone turned to the large screen an image came up in crystal-clear focus.

'That's us,' said Gan at once.

'It's *Liberator*,' Vila confirmed.

Blake glanced at the machine over his shoulder. 'Not much of a prediction,' he said disparagingly. 'Just travelling through space.'

'It is not a prediction,' Orac stated crisply. 'It is an immutable certainty: space vehicle will be destroyed.'

'What!!' Jenna exclaimed.

'You're not given to practical jokes, are you?' Vila said sourly. 'Because that wasn't funny.'

'How soon is this supposed to happen?' asked Blake.

'The event is not far distant.'

'How far distant?'

There was no immediate reply, and Gan said, 'There must be some way of making him tell us when . . . . '

'Be more precise,' Avon told the machine.

'The event is now even less distant,' came the cryptic reply.

Vila looked round at the others. 'I don't believe it.'

'Zen. Systems status?' Jenna asked the master computer.

'*All systems are functioning normally.*'

'But Zen's only a machine,' Vila pointed out.

'So is Orac,' Avon reminded him craftily, removing the activator device. The glow faded and Orac once more resembled nothing more impressive than a box of cast-off components.

Vila sat back, a big delighted grin on his face. 'That's fixed Orac!'

There was a general mood of relief, until Blake's quiet voice said thoughtfully, 'No, it hasn't.'

'What do you mean?' Jenna asked, the smile slipping off her face.

'We're all forgetting one thing.' Blake slowly raised his eyes and looked at the scanner screen. 'The prediction has already been made.'

The huge magnificent spacecraft hung motionless against a glittering spread of diamond-bright stars. Each one of the crew felt an affection for the ship that couldn't be expressed in words. *Liberator* was their home, their refuge in a hostile Universe. It was unthinkable that they would ever lose it.

But the unthinkable happened — just as Orac had predicted.

In front of their horrified, disbelieving eyes the spacecraft disintegrated in a massive fireball that expanded across the heavens, a menacing cloud of destruction blotting out the stars.